T0288546

PENGUIN BOOKS
FOR THE WIN

Catherine Dellosa plays video games for a living, reads comics for inspiration, and writes fiction because she's in love with words. She lives in Manila, Philippines with her husband, whose ideas fuel the fire in her writing.

Her Young Adult fantasy novel, *Of Myths And Men*, has been published by Penguin Random House SEA and is her love letter to gamer geeks, mythological creatures, aliens, and epic quests to save the world. The second book in the trilogy, *Of Life And Lies*, is out now.

When it comes to contemporary YA, *For The Win: The Not-So-Epic Quest Of A Non-Playable Character* is another tribute to gaming, while her light speculative YA romance *The Summer Of Letting Go* is coming soon, also published by PRH SEA.

She has also penned *The Choices We Made (And Those We Didn't)* published by BRUMultiverse, as well as *Raya and Grayson's Guide to Saving the World* and *The Bookshop Back Home* as part of #romanceclass—a community of Filipino authors who are equally in love with words too.

When she's not lost in the land of make-believe, she works as a games journalist for one of the biggest mobile gaming media outlets in the UK. She one day hopes to soar the skies as a superhero, but for now, she strongly believes in saving lives through her works in fiction. Check out her books at bit.ly/catherinedellosabooks, or follow her on FB/IG/Twitter at @thenoobwife.

ADVANCE PRAISE FOR *FOR THE WIN*

'I was utterly charmed by this book! Dellosa perfectly balances the heartwarming and the bittersweet in this delightful coming-of-age story. I fell in love with all the endearing characters, the realistic portrayal of young love, and the inclusion of an inventive video game I'm dying to play IRL! I can't wait for everyone to read this lovely novel about fighting for your dreams, and learning when to let things go.'

—Lena Jeong, author of *And Break The Pretty Kings*

'Perfect for fans of *500 Days of Summer*, this will-they-won't-they young adult story shows that real romance is so much more than playing the game and trying to win the girl. A fast-paced, fun, and meaningful read.'

—E.L. Shen, author of *The Queens of New York and The Comeback*

'*For the Win* is an absolutely charming unrequited love story set in the gaming world. You will root so hard for Nat and his best friend Lena who pop to life, as if you were in an interactive game with them. Grab this book now!'

—Lyn Liao Butler, Amazon bestselling author of *Someone Else's Life*

'*For The Win* is humorous, poignant and unexpected. It is a sweet read laced with tenderness and some sad bits, perfect for YA readers who want something different. I found myself cheering for both Nat and Lena. Wholly recommended!'

—Joyce Chng, author of *Fire Heart*

'Call this "Love in a Time of Warcraft*": like a love story played out over Twitch, with shredded hearts instead of spilled guts (*kickbutt Pinoy edition)'

—Daryl Kho, multiple award-winning and bestselling author of *Mist-Bound: How to Glue Back Grandpa*

'A coming-of-age story that will bring on all the feels, *For The Win* showcases Catherine's wit and finesse in the romance genre, and I guarantee heartstrings will be tugged, and butterflies will be felt.'

—Leslie W, author of *The Night of Legends trilogy*

'A phenomenal love story that keeps tugging at your heart. This is a refreshing YA tale with relatable characters that you will root for immediately. A testimony to Catherine Dellosa's craft in writing romance for teens and character development.'

—Eva Wong Nava, author of *The House of Little Sisters*

'This heartfelt love story is one for the gamers and dreamers. *For the Win* is the complete package with relatable characters, compelling prose, and universal themes of friendship, coming-of-age, and the trials and tribulations of young love.'

—Joyce Chua, author of *Land of Sand and Song*

'Gamer Nathaniel Carpio (Nat) should be the hero in the video game he plays, but lately is feeling more like a Non-Playable Character. Relatable and oozing with charm, *For the Win* is a sweet coming-of-age story that will have you rooting for Nat and his conquests in gaming, love, and in life.'

—Grace K. Shim, author of *The Noh Family*

'You don't need to be a gamer to fall for this fast-paced, gently humorous love story. The plot twist is SO satisfying.'

—Anne Elicaño-Shields, London Writers Award winner

ALSO BY *CATHERINE DELLOSA*

For The Win
The Not-So-Epic Quest
of a Non-Playable Character

Catherine Dellosa

PENGUIN BOOKS

An imprint of Penguin Random House

PENGUIN BOOKS

USA | Canada | UK | Ireland | Australia
New Zealand | India | South Africa | China | Southeast Asia

Penguin Books is part of the Penguin Random House group of companies
whose addresses can be found at global.penguinrandomhouse.com

Published by Penguin Random House SEA Pte Ltd
9, Changi South Street 3, Level 08-01,
Singapore 486361

First published in Penguin Books by Penguin Random House SEA 2023

ISBN 9789815144000

Typeset in Garamond by MAP Systems, Bengaluru, India

www.penguin.sg

To my fellow gamer geeks, always remember: up, up, down, down, left, right, left, right, B, A, Start

Contents

One

In Which the God of the Sun Burns Me to A Crisp and Has a Photo to Prove It

My first day at Tala Tales Games will always be defined by three things: the unlimited buffet spread of nachos, my untimely urge to sneeze right when the photographer was about to take the obligatory group photo, and getting burned to a crisp by the God of the Sun.

Apolaki raises his mighty scythe and his death glare sears through my soul. His face—raw, unbridled fury. His eyes—white-hot balls of fire. His curls—glorious.

I'm totally going to die, and all I can think about is how annoying his perfect hair is.

'I am Sun. I am War. And today is your reckoning.'

I gulp. 'Well, shit.'

Explosions and music and perfectly timed CGI animations and the word 'DEFEAT' flashes mercilessly on my screen. Someone roars like a triumphant war chief coming home with the spoils of battle, and a pretty face pops up from behind the monitor in front of me.

'GG.' A pair of big, bright, charcoal eyes leers at me. 'And so another tribe falls to Relentless_Lena's might. You suck, Nat.'

She puckers her lips with that sideways smirk that always makes my insides squirm. In a good way.

Resistance is futile.

'You got me.' I rub the back of my neck and grin. 'How about *not* using the Diwata Clan for once?'

'No can do, pal. I'm too well-versed in the Diwata's strategic art of kicking your ass.' She whirls her head around and points to a floor-to-ceiling poster on the wall, her messy ponytail bobbing right along behind her. 'Besides, who wouldn't want to use *that?*'

My shoulders slump. I know exactly what she's talking about.

Gigantic and noble and lording over us all, Apolaki poses in a gallant stance on the larger-than-life poster. The God of Sun and War is the main hero of the Diwata Clan, and if you let him get too close to your base, he can single-handedly destroy everything you've ever built and spell immediate doom for your tribe. I personally prefer using the more feral Aswang Clan, but Apolaki is a crowd favourite for players of *Mitolohiya* for a reason. What makes him even more appealing to many is the suave gentleman grinning right alongside the CGI character in the poster.

Rafael Antonio, world-famous Filipino voice actor and notorious in the gaming world as the guy who gets all the 'token noble young hero' parts, lends his vocal chops to *Mitolohiya* as the ever-so-regal Apolaki. He adds a deep and commanding power to the character with a touch of vulnerability, which all the girls love, apparently. They say he brings the hero to life so effing flawlessly, so it's no wonder his video game streaming channel on YouTube has one of the highest numbers of followers in the country.

And Lena, unfortunately, is part of that following.

'All hail Relentless_Lena!' She hums the *Mitolohiya* victory theme like a rock star, and maybe she is. She's bopping her head to an imaginary beat with her face scrunched up and her arms in the air, rogue strands of long frizzy hair sticking out from her ponytail, her plain white shirt all wrinkled from gaming too long. She's still gazing up at the Apolaki poster, the glare from the flickering computer screen flitting around in a soft dance on her face. She has never been more beautiful.

She's weird and wonderful and she's not with me, but all I can think about is how it would feel for her fingers to fill the spaces between mine, not as friends but maybe as something else. Would all these games matter then? Or would it fill this chasm in my chest with different ones and zeroes, with stolen glances and secret smiles, with greasy chicken inasal and oversized sodas and random conversations in the middle of the night?

Seeing her ogling at Rafael's poster yanks me back to where we are right now, crashing down to reality. We've been playing *Mitolohiya* for an hour, lounging around in the cozy lobby of Tala Tales Games HQ.

At the beginning of our senior year, the developer posted a call for applicants who want to pursue a career in video games. The iHubTech Institute is promoting a new game development course for the brightest young minds, and it partnered with Tala Tales Games to scout for said young minds.

The deal is that Tala Tales Games would hold a quick tour-slash-summer camp of sorts with little lectures in between, and the iHubTech Institute would sponsor the qualified applicants' college tuition for the game dev course. I guess Tala Tales Games would obviously be keeping a close eye on those with the biggest potential, and it's a gateway for anyone to land a job here after graduation with the least amount of resistance.

Today is the official photo shoot day. Mom was supposed to pick us up an hour ago, but thankfully, Tala Tales Games' lobby is littered with desktop computers and comfy lounge chairs where anyone can log on and play *Mitolohiya* to their heart's content.

Against Relentless_Lena though, I haven't been doing so well.

Lena leans back into her seat, and I have to get up and walk around my desktop to talk to her. 'I still can't believe we made it this far. There's only what, like, fifty of us left?'

'Forty-nine. One kid was disqualified for plagiarizing his last submission. I heard them talking about it in the pantry.' I cross my arms and lean back against her table. 'There's just that final game concept proposal and essay left, plus the tournament mixer thingy.'

Lena and I have aced the whole application process so far. We didn't have to prove we're great programmers or anything— I guess the company believes that's something you can teach. Plus, it's not just the actual code that makes up a game, they told us. We just have to be interested enough in how a game works and in the game itself, and we have to make an effort whenever we attend the short lectures throughout the programme. I think they're mostly looking for people with the right attitude—those who will fit right into their work culture.

Lena blinks her long lashes at me. 'You'll get in, Nat. They call it a networking night, but everyone knows that it's still a tournament. Whoever wins in that night's "friendly match" will definitely be in the head honchos' sights.'

'In that case, it'll be you. Nobody can cross paths with Relentless_Lena and live to tell the tale.'

'True.' Lena straightens up in her seat. 'Speaking of. Some guy's challenging me.' She squints at the blinking notification on her screen. 'Someone named TheRealApolaki. The nerve.'

'Mom hasn't texted yet, so it could still be a while.' I check my phone and shrug. 'Go for it.'

She squints at the username for a while longer, then promptly accepts the challenge. The loading screen pops up, Diwata Clan vs. Diwata Clan, and Lena grins with that unstoppable twinkle in her eye. 'This guy's about to see who the *real* Apolaki is.'

She rolls her shoulders, straightens her ponytail, and slouches, humped over her keyboard with her hand on the mouse. Here's how I know her first few minutes will go:

1. She licks her lips—her workers have been assigned to their resources on a 1:1 ratio.
2. Her eye twitches—the base's defences are built.
3. She cracks her neck to the left, then to the right—her ground troops are in place.

Pretty soon, she'll be humming the battle theme to herself when she's about to launch an attack—which I've told her time and time again is a dead giveaway of her strategy—then she'll purse her lips sideways, right before she makes her final move. Nobody has probably studied the opponent more than the actual opponent's game strategy than I have.

I mean, I'm not a creep or anything. I just think that Lena is that amazing, and honestly, why would I want to stare at her screen and not at her face?

Okay, so that does come out as creepy.

I lean forward and fix my gaze right on Lena's screen.

Ten minutes in and she's already built her expansions, amassed her troops, and commanded the Diwata Clan's gods and goddesses to scout the map and position themselves right where she wants them to be. The Aswang Clan is known for its melee brawls and brute force skirmishes, while the spirits of the Engkanto Clan fight best where they can cast their powerful magic spells from afar. The Diwata Clan, on the other hand, is a good balance of both, and Lena knows how to maximize each character's skills to land the most impactful death blow.

TheRealApolaki doesn't stand a chance.

No matter how many times I've seen Lena do her thing, it still amazes me how expertly she moves that mouse cursor around all while speed-typing keyboard shortcuts like a boss. I bet her Actions Per Minute is off the charts, and she's not even competing pro.

It doesn't take long before that very same animation of Apolaki's final blow plays out on screen, flashing the word 'VICTORY' in all its euphoric glory.

She bobs her head to the victory music and hums the theme song like she always does with every single win.

I grin. 'I guess TheRealApolaki isn't so real, after all.'

Lena's lips curl into a satisfied smile, and in that tiny space in time, the little drum in my chest starts up again.

Of course, fate picks that exact moment for a looming shadow to march right up to us. 'Relentless_Lena?' asks a deep, suave baritone.

We turn around.

Standing there in all his YouTube-subscriber-hoarding glory, Rafael Antonio extends his hand out to Lena, all fresh and unfazed and smiling at her with his perfect set of dazzling white teeth.

I watch as Lena's big, round eyes grow even bigger, her cheeks flushed and her smile just as wide. She takes the online celebrity's hand and keeps her gaze locked on his face, completely forgetting about unremarkable little me standing right there beside her. 'Umm. Hi.'

'You just mopped the enchanted floors of *Mitolohiya* with my Diwata troops.' Rafael Antonio chuckles, making Lena blush even harder. I don't even know why they're still holding hands. I mean, handshakes aren't supposed to last that long, right? It takes all of my self-control not to karate-chop their hands apart. And maybe even hit Rafael Antonio in the face a little bit too.

Then, in the flesh, the real, *real* Apolaki tells her the words that will mark this moment in history as the moment I lose Lena completely.

'You wanna go grab some lunch?'

* * *

'So, how'd the photo shoot go?' Dad leans against the counter and turns to me, just as I accidentally bang on the cash register drawer so hard that the coins inside rattle like it's New Year's Eve.

He eyes the drawer, then my frowning face. 'O–kay . . . so it *didn't* go well?'

'Sorry,' I mumble. 'It was all right.'

Dad peers over the counter at the three rows of desktop computers in front of us. 'Where's Lena?'

'You're not going to get an answer out of him, hon.' Mom swings by the counter with a smirk. 'I've been asking him the same thing since I picked him up this morning, and all I got was a look that could cut through lead.'

I shoot her a death glare.

'There. That one.' Mom nods at my face and chuckles, disappearing toward the back exit of the shop.

'Ah. Guess that explains the ruthless attack on the cash register.' Dad's desperately trying to bite back a grin. 'You two had a fight?'

'Can we not talk about this? Josh is coming over any second.' Not to mention I was just rendered invisible by an online celebrity a while back. I mean, I'm pretty proud of my messy hair. I got that from my father, who was apparently a 'real looker' back in the day. We both have that 'just rolled out of bed' look my mother loves so much—then again, since she's the source of all these compliments, her opinions probably aren't too reliable.

Still, no amount of adorably dishevelled hair can top whatever Rafael Antonio has, apparently.

'Of course, of course.' Dad raises both hands. 'We're still not done with these expense reports, though. This stuff is Business Survival 101. Gotta show you the ropes in case your old man bites, you know.'

Ever since Dad spoke to one of my teachers at my graduation ceremony, and she told him about that weird chest pain her husband got that morning (I mean, why would they even talk about that thing? Adults.), he's been obsessed with 'showing the ropes' and hoping to pass along this little shop-that-could to his 'sole heir'. He's also been stressing out about how to drive more customers to the shop and make it thrive even more just for me.

Just in case he gets that weird chest pain too. Just in case he doesn't wake up in the morning. Or just in case I wake up in the morning and he's no longer there.

'Sure, Dad. Assets and liabilities. Can we pick up where we left off later tonight?'

'An assets-and-liabilities date it is.' Dad's eyes twinkle. 'Feel free to take Unit 23.'

Right on cue, Josh pushes the glass door plastered with old video game posters and saunters into the computer rental shop, the chimes tinkling happily overhead. He grins at my father behind the counter. 'Hey, Mr C.'

'Joshua!' Dad grins right back. 'Are you hitting 50,000 subscribers today?'

Josh waves his flash drive at him. 'I'll try.'

I slink out from behind the counter and lead Josh to Unit 23, and as we wait for the computer to boot up, I plop down on the unoccupied unit beside him.

'Can you?' I ask. 'Hit 50K?'

'Maybe.' Josh plugs the flash drive into the USB port. 'I'm feeling good about this one, Nat. A full set of random Avengers figurines. Series comparisons, stock availability, the works. Today just might be the day.'

He boots up the video editing software and starts working his magic, once again making me wish I had some other technical skill aside from just being a good gamer. On top of his sick video editing skills, Josh also knows how to work a crowd, and his unboxing YouTube channel is proof of that.

I know he's applying for a graphic design course in college, but honestly, does he need it? Right now, he's a mere 500 followers away from hitting the 50,000-subscriber mark. I still can't believe that many people are watching him open boxes of random toys and action figures just for the heck of it.

Then again, Josh a.k.a. bulk_smash doesn't understand my love for video games either, but that doesn't mean we can't still be best friends.

'When you hit 50K, will you be showing off your face?' I grin. 'You know, live the proper celebrity life and all that?'

'No way, man. The great bulk_smash values his anonymity above all else,' he says. 'Besides, I don't think Bea would approve of that kind of life for me.'

'Afraid of all the attention?'

'Totally. I mean, I don't want to be Rafael Antonio over there.' Josh points to a poster of Apolaki on the wall in front of us. Posters and ads from all kinds of games are up on the cramped walls of our internet cafe, and unfortunately, Apolaki-slash-Rafael's face comes with the territory. 'Well, maybe a little. Subscriber-wise. I'd kill to have his kind of following.'

'It's funny you should mention him.' I sigh. 'I sorta ran into him today.'

Josh turns his eyes away from the panels of his storyboard on the screen. 'You ran into Rafael Antonio? At the Tala Tales photo shoot?'

'Yeah. He . . . played *Mitolohiya* at the lobby.'

'That's pretty awesome. I would have asked him all these questions on how to be the ultimate YouTube star.' Josh's eyes are shining. 'So, what happened? You had a session with him or something?'

'He asked Lena out to lunch.'

'Oh.' Josh's face falls. 'That sucks.'

'Yeah.'

When Lena and I met four years ago, Josh was right there with me, peering over my shoulder into my monitor at the online auction. I was locked in a bidding war with some girl over official Tala Tales Games merchandise—a replica of half of Bathala's *agimat*, which comes with a special code for exclusive in-game equipment—and I was almost at the price limit that Dad gave me over the thing. I was pissed and desperate, the clock was ticking, and I only had a few minutes left before I lost the bid, so I sent my nemesis a message to try and bargain for it like a coward. The girl did *not* give in, won the bid, and even lectured me generously about how she deserved to win because she was the ultimate *Mitolohiya* fan.

She also turned out to be a nice person, online war freak nature aside. Since then, Elena Dizon and I have been inseparable, hanging out after class at the sidewalk grillery where our schools are nearest and playing games here at our shop whenever we have the chance.

And then, after a particularly bad day in school and against the rainy backdrop of the fading sun, she fished for change in her pocket at the sidewalk grillery and handed me a 'six-peso coin'—a five and a one stuck together, inseparable, ridiculous. She told me she had been holding onto it for a while as a special charm and was her most prized possession at the moment, but she gave it to me, just because she wanted me to feel better.

'It's silly, I know, but you mean that much to me,' she said.

There was no room for silliness then, no time to wonder why my heart was clawing against my chest, no way to rationalize the fear that gripped me with panic so intense that I had to clench my fist to steel myself.

Because the rain had stopped and the water hung in the air like mist. The vapour framed Lena's face in an ethereal glow, and the moment held nothing and everything at the same time.

The six-peso coin had done it. The smile that I was so used to seeing every day suddenly looked different—tugging at my heart and radiating an unsettling warmth from within.

To this day, I still don't understand how someone can just be your friend and then you wake up one day and all of a sudden she's something else. But I guess I've always liked her from the very first time we met—it just had to take another random act of kindness on her part to admit that to myself.

'Sorry, man.' Josh pulls me back to the present, staring at me with his video draft forgotten. The expression on my face must have looked absolutely defeated because he plants both hands on my shoulders.

'Nathaniel Carpio. So Lena met her online crush—no big deal,' he says. 'It's just lunch, right? It's not like they're getting married.'

I've always thought that Lena and I are meant to be together. One of my favourite console games of all time features an adventure-hunting couple named Nathan Drake and Elena Fisher, and I just . . . well . . . how can Lena and I not be the same thing, you know?

'I guess you're right.' I glare at the Apolaki poster. 'It's probably just a one-off thing. A celebrity trying to look good for the press.'

But because fate wants to take my stupid Nathan-and-Elena dream, trample it on the ground, and then rub the mangled pieces in my face, the messaging app on my phone sends me a notification.

It's a selfie. Lena is grinning from ear to ear at the camera, and right there, with his arm casually draped around her like they've been together since the dawn of time, is Rafael Antonio enjoying their no-big-deal lunch.

Along with the photo, Lena has sent me a message that makes me wish I myself had burned up under the wrath of the Sun God instead of just my avatar this morning. 'We're hanging out again tomorrow! THIS IS THE BEST DAY OF MY ENTIRE LIFE.'

Josh takes one look at my screen and curses. 'Nat. Nat. You okay? Hey . . .'

But Josh's voice fades farther and farther away. Oddly enough, the message feels like an unwelcome splash of ice-cold water, jolting me out of my complacency and forcing my mind to zero in with laser focus.

Because at that moment of complete and utter clarity, my very being commits itself to a singular mission, and no, despite how charming the Big Boss is, defeat is *not* an option.

I have to destroy Rafael Antonio, level up, and win Elena Dizon's heart.

Stage One: Destroy Rafael Antonio

Two

In Which I Blame the Lag
For Ruining Everything

'And then I got him to talk about that new *Mitolohiya* expansion pack and I was all "whaaat?" and he was like, "hell yes", and I swear I died right there.'

'Uh-huh.' I'm mesmerized by a persistent fly trying to sneak its way into the soy sauce bottle across from me.

Lena tugs at a piece of barbecue skewers with her teeth, waving her stick around. 'He's got all of these upcoming projects, so it's a lucky coincidence that we caught him at the lobby yesterday. He's only going to be in town for a month to wrap up with some of Apolaki's voice work for the new campaigns.'

'Okay.' The fly gives up and hovers over a piece of grilled squid on the plate of the guy beside me.

'He also told me all about what goes on behind the scenes, you know? And that part's the most interesting for me, honestly. I mean, I've always been curious about what goes on in the recording booths and how all the sound mixing works. I was kinda thinking, maybe, someday I'd show them some of the stuff I've been working on. Or maybe I should make an official demo reel. *If* I get the guts to.' Lena goes on, 'Did I mention we're meeting up again this afternoon? I hope I get a backstage pass. I'd *kill* for that.'

15

The guy beside me stands up from the long bar table we're all sitting on, and the fly promptly buzzes away. 'That's great.'

Lena exaggerates a loud sigh and unceremoniously pokes my arm with her barbecue stick.

'Hey! What gives?'

'You've been more interested in that stupid fly than in anything I've been saying for the past fifteen minutes.' She wrinkles her nose. 'Did you even hear a word I've said?'

'Of course, I did. Expansion pack, additional voiceovers, Rafael Antonio's here for a month. Did you know he used to be a talking trash can?' I swivel my elevated bar stool to face Lena. I did some research last night, staying up way too late browsing through his previous roles just to dig up any dirt I can find on the guy. If I'm going to destroy him, I need to have enough ammo to do it. 'Humiliating. Not exactly the dignified hero you'd expect him to be.'

'Raf told me about that!' Lena giggles like it's the most adorable thing. 'It was his first gig, and he was willing to do anything at eighteen. Fast forward years later and he's one of the biggest names in the VA community, with an upcoming unnamed project at Square Enix. *Square Enix*!' She squeals, making a few heads in the small open-air sidewalk grillery turn toward her. 'A long way from a talking trash can, huh? It's all hush-hush though, that Square Enix thing. They'll announce the big reveal at The Game Awards next year.'

'Oh. Cool.' Damn it, that thing backfired. And she calls him *Raf* now? 'What time are you guys meeting up? Are we still on for the mall later?'

'Oh definitely. I need to run a few errands for Dad anyway.'

'Cool,' I repeat. 'A new batch of wireless earbuds just came in. They're supposed to send signals to your brain to help you focus.'

'The future is here,' she grins. 'I never thought anything else would come after Active Noise Cancellation.'

'Today, it's brain signals. Tomorrow, mind control.'

Lena clutches her head and makes an awkward whirring noise, then we both burst out laughing. Thanks to this guy I know at the Sound-E-Scapes store down at the local mall, I get the first news every time a new shipment of audio equipment drops. It's been a habit of mine for years now to take Lena there to sample all the new merch before anyone else does, because the guy who runs the shop owes me a favour—I won a *Mitolohiya* mini-contest for him where the prize was official Engkanto gear.

I've been doing this as her friend because Lena is such an audiophile, even before I realized I liked her—sadly, I don't think it holds enough weight these days. It doesn't seem to be anywhere near what *Raf* can apparently do for her now.

I swallow the lump in my throat. 'Where are you guys headed later?'

'Dunno. Just somewhere nearby, I guess. I've been meaning to try out that new milk tea place down the street.' Lena shrugs. 'He's low-key that way, you know, for a celebrity. You should meet him sometime, Nat. He's pretty great.'

I grit my teeth. 'Maybe.' And then an idea comes to me. 'Why don't you invite him to the internet cafe?'

'Hmm. You think?' Lena plays with her ponytail, which she'll probably drown in shampoo before she goes to bed tonight. She's always complaining about the grill smoke getting caught in her strands, effectively making her hair smell like chicken inasal all day. It's still one of our favourite hangouts anyway, with the greasy countertop, the five-item menu taped to the wall with the laminate peeling at the corners, and the fake-leather bar stools weakly protected with a smudged plastic sheet. Plus, Lena always picks the seat right next to the grimy stainless exhaust, just because she thinks the smoke makes everything more delicious.

I hate that I know all these things about her.

'You think your parents won't mind?' Lena says. 'Once word gets out, it might get crowded.'

'That's fine.' I pick at an invisible lint on my shoulder. 'It'll be good for business. Dad will probably go out and spread the word himself, the way he's been crunching numbers like crazy lately. I'm sure *Raf* will be okay with it. It's for his fans, after all—unless he's secretly a jerk or something.'

'"Rafael Antonio Makes Surprise Appearance at Local Internet Café." I can already see the swarm of new customers.' Lena yanks out her phone. 'I'll text him right now.'

I try not to linger on the fact that Lena can just randomly text him on his personal mobile number, which he probably doesn't just give away to random strangers. But then again, it's Lena— who wouldn't want to give her their number?

Focus, Nat. If I want my plan to work, I have to make sure Raf shows up at the shop first.

'He's in. I just sent him the location on Google Maps.' Lena grins. 'You're brilliant, Nat.'

I grin back. *You have no idea.*

* * *

Carpio Diem Internet Café (my Dad thinks he's hilarious) is just thirty desktop computers and lots and lots of posters on the wall. The banged-up air-conditioner keeps sputtering like it's the end of the world, and in a tropical country where the heat index just gets higher and higher each day, no amount of cooling systems can ever be enough. Three rickety stand fans are holding on for dear life to help with the temperature to no avail, but thankfully, the shop rarely ever gets too crowded. Most days, the cubicles aren't even fully occupied, making the stuffy shop bearable even in the height of summer.

But today is not like most days.

Today, Rafael Antonio is standing in the middle of Carpio Diem in casual jeans and a shirt that says 'Keep Calm and Call a

Diwata'. Even as all the fanboys and fangirls inside the cramped internet café are itching to grab a selfie with him or to have him sign everything from mouse pads to used table napkins, he's still as calm and composed as ever, not a strand out of place from his brushed up black hair, not a bead of sweat on his brow.

I hate that he doesn't seem to function like a normal human being.

But while everyone else is ogling over the YouTube star, my eyes are focused only on Lena, whose white Tala Tales Games commercial shirt that's two sizes too big has a small barbecue stain on the hem. I'm strangely attracted to the stray strands of hair sticking to the damp skin on the back of her neck.

Somehow, there's a different kind of heat inside me.

Lena spots me in the crowd and her dark grey eyes brighten. I indulge myself with the idea that, in a sea of random strangers, it's a look that's reserved just for me.

'There you are.' She weaves through the fans and grabs my arm. 'When I saw Mr and Mrs Carpio doing crowd control outside, I thought you were out there with them.'

I let her drag me behind her without a word until she practically shoves me into Raf in the middle of the crowd.

'Ah, you must be Nathaniel,' Raf flashes his pearly whites at me and extends his hand, ignoring the fans threatening to consume us at any minute. 'Sorry, we didn't get a proper introduction yesterday. Lena's told me all about you.'

Has she, now? I shake his hand. 'Likewise.'

'Thanks for inviting me out here,' Raf gestures around us and throws me a sheepish smile. 'Anything for the fans, but I have to apologize to your parents for the clean-up in advance.'

Damn it, this guy's charming. 'No biggie. If you'd seen the way my dad's been acting since he heard the news this morning, you'd probably feel differently.' I take a deep breath. Here goes nothing. 'So, Raf. You wanna fight?'

His winning smile falters. 'Excuse me?'

'A match. On *Mitolohiya*. Just a friendly one-on-one.' I clench my fists to my sides to keep them from shaking, hoping Lena wouldn't notice. 'You know, for the fans.'

And just like that, he blinks his confusion away. 'Oh! Sure, man. That'd be awesome.' He winks at Lena with an easy nod, and she blushes. Again. 'I need to bounce back from yesterday's humiliating wipe-out, after all.'

'Okay. Cool.'

At the prospect of a real-time battle, the mini crowd inside the shop buzzes with even more excitement. Raf and I sit across from each other, and immediately, everyone takes sides behind either one of us. I feel like the shop is going to explode at any minute.

When Lena finds a spot behind my left shoulder, it almost makes me want to shoot up and declare a win right there.

'So, Nat.' Raf peers at me over the top of his monitor. 'You have a preference for the Diwata Clan like Relentless_Lena over there?'

'The Aswang are more my thing,' I reply as the loading screen pops up. There's a quick animated intro, the peaceful lands of *Mitolohiya* blanketed by an invisible enchantment that conceals them from the human world. But when a salamangkero—a conjurer of sorts—discovers a chink in the armour and opens up a portal for the humans to cross over to the other side, all three tribes of the *Mitolohiya* lands have to rise up and defend their homeland threatened by the conquering forces of the humans from the outside. Of course, as in most drawn-out wars, the factions ended up stirring discord and destruction among all the clans in the process, and all three tribes have been warring with each other ever since.

It's epic. It's magical. It's the most awesome way I can prove I'm the better player.

By the end of this whole thing, Lena and the rest of the crowd will cheer and celebrate my sweeping victory, and Lena will forget all about effing pretty boy on the other side of the monitor.

'You got this, Nat,' Lena whispers in my ear, and in that split-second, the heat and the crowd and the stuffy shop all fade away, and it's just me and Lena, her soft hand on my shoulder and her chicken inasal ponytail and the barbecue stain on her shirt.

The *Mitolohiya* theme song blares from the speakers in front of me, and I have to tear my eyes away from Lena's smiling eyes as she hums the theme under her breath.

Raf and I put our headphones on. *Here we go.*

There's a small whopping and clapping around us as the game starts, and right off the bat, I get an in-game message from Guest_Computer_19 that says, 'GLHF :)'.

I send the message right back, even though I have absolutely no intention of wishing him 'good luck' or wanting him to 'have fun'.

After spawning enough Duwende to farm minerals in my base, I send out a few Sigbin—in and out, fast, and efficient—to scout my surroundings in stealth. The canine-like creatures speed across the map with their humanoid faces bowed low to the ground, their fangs bared and their claws scraping through the earth. The randomly generated map for today's match is a snowy battlefield, and my base is stationed on top of a cliff that juts out from a rocky ravine below. Two snow-capped hills bottleneck the main entrance to my base, which makes for the perfect defensive position. I'm hoping Raf's base isn't as naturally fortified.

I got this.

From Raf's old videos, he's usually too focused on buffing up his main base that he often expands too late, right when his opponent has already built expansions and secured enough resources for the long haul. If I want to rub this win in his face, I have to expand as soon as possible and block off his supplies.

I build my second base nearby while spawning two Tikbalang sentinels to stand guard over the bottleneck bridge into my main base. The siege units tower over my base, their horse heads scanning the entrance with fiery, pitch-black eyes. Their muscular human torsos are just as menacing as their lower bodies that taper off into powerful, supercharged hooves.

I got this.

When I have a handful of big, fat, Bangungot bruiser tanks and a group of speedy Manananggal for some serious Damage Per Second, I activate the research facility to upgrade my ground Manananggal to flying units. The femme fatales strip off from their legs and hover above my base with their entrails hanging from their waists, as enormous bat-like wings sprout from their backs simultaneously. Right then, I get an attack alert.

The Sigbin I've been micromanaging to scout around are under fire.

I switch my view over to the lower part of the battlefield map and see that my Sigbin have made it to the entrance to Raf's base, and two Lambana units—small, glowing, forest fairies—zap them to oblivion. Forest deities can only mean one thing—Raf has a Maria Makiling hero unit somewhere this early in the game, and her Lambana troops can cause massive Area of Effect damage with a single skill alone.

I got this?

Right before I'm set to send out my first attack wave, a small commotion over on Raf's side makes me look up from my screen. The fans watching from behind him are murmuring excitedly to themselves, hiding smiles behind hands and sneaking glances at me.

That can't be good.

The moment I send out my Manananggal for an offensive attack on Raf's base, his units pop right up behind me like he knows exactly what I'm up to.

And all hell breaks loose.

My main base, weakly defended because I spent my resources on expansion rather than fortifying my main command post, crumbles under the might of a mere three-woman team from his tribe. Mayari, Hana, and Tala—daughters of the god Bathala—sweep into my base effortlessly, tossing my two Tikbalang sentinels aside like mere ragdolls. And because my all-too-powerful attack force is already halfway through the map when my base was invaded, I can't recall them to base in time to defend it.

I have no idea how this could have happened. He's never done a risky Diwata rush like this, this early in the game. I swear I had Raf's strategies down pat.

In a last-ditch attempt to defend my base, I transform my main command post into its defensive position, revealing the gigantic Bakunawa serpent coiled underneath the ground as a stationary defence. But even that doesn't do shit.

It doesn't take long before my structures are decimated. This time, Apolaki didn't even need to make an appearance.

The fans behind Raf cheer as soon as the 'DEFEAT' banner flashes on my screen, and he stands. 'Good game.' He throws me an easy-going grin, before promptly turning his attention back to his adoring fans.

I slump there in my seat with my hands all clammy, the loss still not sinking in.

Lena squeezes my shoulder and gently plucks my headphones off. 'You did good, Nat. That was a bold move, what he did.' She half-shrugs like it's no big deal, like it's just a friendly game between two *Mitolohiya* players, like I didn't just lose the definitive battle for her heart.

As she gravitates over to Raf, I accept the harsh reality that my ultimate mission to destroy Rafael Antonio isn't off to a very good start.

Three

In Which Diwatas Whip My Ass and Post It On Social Media

I press the button labelled 'Cappuccino', and the machine makes this odd whirring sound before the coffee drips down to my cup on the dispenser. I stare at it like it holds the meaning of life.

Lena always said that waiting for drip coffee is life's greatest irony, when you're itching to get going and grab your caffeine fix, but the universe makes you go through this torturous wait. 'It's the lost art of patience,' she said to me once. 'Like the slow build-up to the climax of a good song. One moment you're trying to extract the emotion from the melody, and the next moment, it's right there, and it's so great and enchanting and the wait kind of makes the crescendo more beautiful, don't you think?'

'Are you done?' The guy behind me taps his foot. I jolt back to my senses.

'Uh, just one more.' I replace the just-brewed cappuccino with an empty cup. 'Sorry.'

Mr Impatient grunts and stomps right out of the 7-Eleven. Guess he would rather give up on coffee altogether than wait in line for two more minutes.

I hit the 'French Vanilla' button and pay for the two drinks at the cashier.

'I thought you'd drowned yourself in caffeine,' Mom grins at me as I approach our bar table with the coffee cups. 'Is hanging out with your mother in public that much of a pain?'

I settle down beside her. 'Why do you always give me such a hard time?'

'Because you make it so easy, sweetheart.' She takes the lid off the cappuccino cup and lets her coffee cool for a bit. 'The sermon today was something, wasn't it?'

Church is a short fifteen-minute walk from our house, and during the homily, the priest went on and on about all the different kinds of love and how there should be no fear in it and everything. Even after Mom and I crossed the street from the church to this 7-Eleven a while back, I can still hear the sermon ringing in my ears.

'I didn't understand a word,' I say, as Mom hands me a freshly steamed siopao bun. No fear in love—how is that even possible?

'We can talk about it, you know.'

I take a bite. 'Talk about what?'

'Your feelings for Lena.'

I almost choke on the asado. 'What?'

'Oh, sweetie. You're the most obvious little thing.' Mom takes a bite from her own siopao bun and smiles. 'When Rafael Antonio was in our shop that day, I saw you after the match. You were just sitting there, slumped in your seat like a wounded baby bird.'

I sip on my coffee and let the thought simmer for a while. 'They're still talking about it.'

'What do you mean?'

I pull out my phone and show her the posts. Some girl from the shop snapped a photo right after Raf's big win, and he reposted it to his gigantic fan base. Now everyone is talking about it, Raf casually hanging out in town and how he really is the real Apolaki, crushing noobs like me like it's nobody's business.

The worst part of it all is that Lena is right there in the photo, rapt attention and a sparkle in her eyes, as Raf grins at her beside him.

'Well. That explains the sudden influx of new customers lately.' Mom looks up from my phone. 'Lena knows about this photo, right?'

'Yes. No. Maybe. I honestly don't know.' I stare out into the sidewalk through the glass panel in front of us. 'She's been hanging out with Raf a lot lately. I haven't seen her much.'

'Come to think of it, weren't you two supposed to have breakfast together a while ago? Something about an e-sports movie marathon of some sort? I overheard you and Josh planning it a few days ago.'

'Yeah, but Raf called to say there was a brunch thingy at the studio, and she wanted to go, so.'

'So, you cancelled your plans.'

'Yes.'

'And you didn't tell her you had them.'

'No.'

'Sweetie.'

'It's okay. I'm supposed to read up on a few basic programming stuff, anyway.' We don't say anything for a while. 'How was the last interview, Mom? I made sure the schedule fits yours just right.'

'It was . . . okay,' she says. 'I think the manager thought I was a little overqualified, to be honest.'

'You're a shoo-in, Mom. I had a pretty good feeling about this one when I submitted your application.' I smile at her. 'And if not, I've still got a bunch of good ones lined up. I'll work on a few of them some more tonight. We'll find something.'

'You're sweet, Nat. You know how hopeless I am with all this online stuff, but I don't want you using up all your time for this.'

I shake my head. 'I'm happy to do it.'

Mom sips her coffee. 'Lena's birthday is coming up, isn't it? You mentioned taking a day off to your father this morning.'

'Yeah. It's the first afternoon in a while that I get her to myself. I sorta made sure of that.' I pause. 'Sorry. That didn't come out right.'

'You're acting like wanting to spend time with your best friend on her birthday is a crime,' she chuckles. 'Let me tell you this. Rafael Antonio may be a big celebrity, but he's not the one she has known all her life, is he? He doesn't know anything real about her, and neither does she know anything real about him.'

I watch as a little girl selling sampaguita garlands sits down on the sidewalk outside, taking shelter from the sweltering summer heat.

'It wasn't love at first sight with your father, you know. Even though he was always as dashing and debonair as he is now.' Mom giggles, reminding me for the hundredth time how lucky she is to have married her best friend. 'It takes work, being in a relationship, because you may want very different things. But you don't have to force yourself to be someone else, either. We raised you better than that.'

I rub the back of my neck and don't say a word.

'How's that essay coming along, by the way?'

Apart from the game concept proposal, the final requirement for the Tala Tales Games scholarship programme is an essay answering the question, 'What motivates you?' It should be simple enough, but it's still there, a blank draft on my computer with a hopeless blinking cursor, and I have no idea how to begin.

'I haven't started.'

'Hmm.' Mom fixates on her coffee in deep thought, making me wonder if she's going to launch into a full-blown lecture as to why I'm slacking off and throwing my future away. But then again, she has never been the lecturing type.

Instead, she asks me an existential-crisis-inducing question that knocks me off my feet.

'Sweetie. What is it that you really want?'

'Um. Another siopao?'

'In life.' Mom clasps her hands in her lap. 'What is it that you really want in life?'

'Erm. Well, since I assume we're still talking about my essay, the scholarship, I guess. I want that scholarship.'

Mom keeps staring at me, completely serious and completely freaking me out. 'And what if you don't get it?'

What? 'Nice pep talk, Mom.'

She ignores my nonsense. 'Does that scare you, honey? Is it frightening not to achieve your goal? For things to go the other way? For things to change?'

And all of a sudden, this image of Lena slipping away from me appears, of Raf with his arm around her, ready to whisk her away, away from this life, away from me.

'Yeah,' I whisper. 'It scares me a whole damn lot.'

She doesn't reply. Instead, she throws me this weird, sympathetic look, the kind you give to someone you know is going to screw everything up and there's nothing you can do about it.

'Can I ask you something, sweetie?' she smiles, and I nod. 'All these years with Lena . . . how come you never made a move?'

I don't like how this conversation is going.

'Were you so afraid of things changing that you got too complacent?' Mom is relentless. 'Did it have to take a certain Rafael Antonio to come into the picture before you felt threatened?'

I grit my teeth.

Just then, like the universe wants to save me from the harsh truth that I'm in denial over, Lena sends me a text message: 'Need to pick something up at the mall before the press launch. Wanna come?'

Mom sneaks a glance at the text and clears her throat. 'Well, Nat, if you need any help with your essay, just holler. The summer's not going to last forever, sweetie.'

I nod.

She finishes up her meal and hands me the canvas tote bag filled with fresh mangoes we bought from the church vendor earlier. 'Anyway, make sure you get these to Lena's father tonight.' She slides down from our bar table and pats my cheek. 'It'll be okay, kiddo. You'll be okay.'

Somehow, I know she's not talking about me walking to the train station alone.

'Thanks, Mom.'

'Mmm-hmm.' And with that, she heads out the 7-Eleven. Outside, I see her stoop down to the sampaguita girl and hand her a fresh siopao bun, before crossing the street toward the bank to pay some bills. Nobody is clamouring to hire a middle-aged ex-balloon-supplier employee despite her best efforts, so I get more of these little days off with her recently.

I contemplate the swirling coffee in my cup and sigh. Mom was right about me and Raf, though. On one hand, I do feel threatened; but on the other hand, I do know everything about Lena. How she prefers Ministop's fried chicken over KFC, how she hates people who don't fall into a single line while waiting for a cubicle at the restroom. How abandoned PLDT phone booths make her sad, how she loves spending time with me at this very table just watching the people go by outside.

She'd make up stories about them and wonder where each person was going, in a great big rush for a meeting, a party, or a date. She'd hum a little tune under her breath, a different one for each person, imagining it is the soundtrack to their lives.

Sometimes, she'd get a random burst of inspiration from all the people-watching, and she'd rush home and tinker with her movie trailers. She'd replace the audio and splice in some music from a different clip, trying to tell her own story through the magic of sound. I'd look at her work and I'd be so damn proud because she's a genius and she's amazing and she's my friend.

Lena turns eighteen tomorrow. There are no fancy parties, no huge gifts, no coming-of-age activities lined up for her. It's up to me to make her feel special, because if anyone in the world deserves to feel that way, it's Lena. And all I need to do is be myself.

I sigh.

The thing is, I'm no voice actor bigshot, and I don't think being me will ever be enough.

* * *

I stare at the huge poster looming over me inside the video game store, and Apolaki glowers right back. He's got his arm raised high into the heavens, a blazing ball of fire scorching through the sky from his open palm, his eyes as fiery as his obvious desire to burn whoever stands in his way.

Which, in this case, is me, apparently.

My eyes wander down the text at the bottom of the poster. Apolaki expansion pack. Coming soon.

Lovely.

'Whoa, Nat! Take a look at this!'

I stop scowling at the poster and squeeze through the cramped aisles of the store toward where Lena is, crouched in front of a shelf stacked with marked-down items. She waves a Blu-ray disc box at me, her eyes twinkling.

'Half off, Nat! And it comes with a Minifig! How cute is that?' Lena flips the box and scans the description of the LEGO game at the back. 'Over fifty characters you can unlock. Sweeeet.'

'Yeah, that's pretty cool.' I browse through the bargain bin with her, knowing full well we will walk out of here empty-handed anyway like we always do. We make sure we stop by this store every time we're at the mall and spend a good chunk of our time just squealing over the titles on display, but we rarely ever buy anything. When budget is an issue, saving up for *Mitolohiya* add-ons is our number one priority.

When Lena feels like we've rummaged enough, we scoot over to the exit, but not before bumping into a kid asking about PlayStation credits at the counter. The store is tiny, but gamers find it pretty charming, so it's almost always packed. Lena and I don't mind.

Once we're out and about, we stroll down the mall looking for something to do. When we hopped off the train a while back, Lena picked up a small paper bag of something she apparently ordered at this kiosk on the second level that personalizes trinkets. I didn't see what it was, and she didn't talk about it, so I didn't ask. I thought she'd want to head to this press launch thing that Raf invited us to right after, but she wanted us to wander around for a bit, and I'm not going to be the idiot who refuses to hang out with her.

Oh, right. There's this small pre-release dinner for the *Mitolohiya* expansion pack tonight, totally private, totally press only. But Raf being Raf sent us both invites, even though I'm pretty sure it's Relentless_Lena he wants to hang out with, and I'm just along for the ride.

The private event would've been the coolest thing in the world if only Raf weren't in the picture.

'Thanks, Nat,' Lena tells me after a while. 'I just need to wander around for a bit. Clear my head.'

'Is everything okay?'

'Dad was drinking more than usual this morning, and when I coaxed an answer out of him, he told me that Mom called.'

'Damn.'

'Yeah.' Lena's hair is loose today, and she tucks a few strands behind her ear. 'He didn't tell me why she called, but he usually drinks more when he's stressed, and she's the only reason he's ever stressed. I love Dad to bits, so when something like this happens . . .' She inches closer to me. It takes everything I have not to casually brush my hand against hers. 'It's just . . . my mom sucks, you know?'

'I know,' I reply. 'And I'm so, so sorry she does.'

Lena sighs. 'I just keep thinking about how she left, like she just full-on chased her dreams and followed her damn *heart*, without any regard for anything or anyone she might leave behind in the dust. There are so many things I *want* to do, Nat, and so many things I *need* to do. I just don't want to end up like her.'

'You're not your mother, Lena, and you're not *Ate* Ami either, if that's what you're thinking. You don't have to give up everything just to get what you want. And if there's anyone who can figure it out, it's you.'

She pauses to stare at me for a while, and I stop walking. Then, she rolls her eyes. 'Cheesy.' She nudges my shoulder. 'Giving pep talks isn't very becoming of an Aswang commander.'

'The mark of a true Aswang.' I feel weightless. 'Crunchy on the outside, soft and cheesy on the inside. They're pretty much just misunderstood. I mean, a Sigbin can very well be man's best friend, you know? They'd make awesome pets.'

'If you don't count the clawing your face off and the bloodsucking and the penchant for terrorizing cattle, sure, they'd make great pets.'

'Hey, they just want to be loved. Aswang have hearts too.'

'If you say so.' Lena's voice is bubbly, and we start back down the hallways again until we reach Sound-E-Scapes. Lena takes her time flitting about the testing section, zipping here and there, trying out different headphones and bopping her head along to the beat I can't hear. She closes her eyes from time to time, the hint of a smile dancing on her lips, and in the sea of shoppers around her, she lights up the entire store. For me, at least.

But every small gesture she makes just proves all the more that she belongs to this great, big world out there, this world of opportunities and music and life.

Her every move is proof that she's not mine.

I busy myself with the power banks and Bluetooth speakers and phone cases on the shelves for a bit, until Lena comes up to me.

'I think I'm ready to go now.'

I nod.

The train station is a little less of a warzone at the moment, and strips of orange streak across the sky over the horizon. Lena suggests an outdoor siomai stand at the bridgeway between the mall exit and the entrance to the station.

'Shoot. They're out of chilli.' Lena frowns at the condiments in the corner of the vendor's cart after she masterfully whips up her sauce combination. I know exactly how she likes it done, her four pieces of siomai swimming in a pool of soy sauce, each steamed ball cut in half with calamansi squeezed into the centre. Then, she will pop some chilli on top of each half like a gourmet chef; only, this time, they're out of chilli.

Which is a shame for me. I don't do soy sauce and calamansi— just sprinkle some chilli powder on mine, and I'm a happy camper.

Lena turns to me with her eyebrows squished together. 'Sorry. We should've picked a different stall.'

'No biggie.' *All I care about is spending time with you.*

We hobble to a secluded corner of the station with our siomai trays in hand and dig in. Lena indulges in a little bit of people-watching for a while, humming under her breath as she eats.

'I'm always listening, always learning,' she told me once, when she was showing me a new trailer with her very own spliced audio. 'But the thing is, you have to listen with your heart, not your ears. Which is super hard for me to do.'

I was in awe of her talent then, and I still am today.

'Want my last piece?' Lena jolts me back to the present, offering her siomai tray to me. 'I probably shouldn't have ordered four pieces. I'll ruin my appetite for dinner.'

'You, finally full?' I chuck my empty siomai tray in the nearby trash bin and tug at my shirt to feign nonchalance. 'No more room left in that bottomless pit you call a tummy?'

She grins, a challenging glint in her eye. 'Don't.'

'Has a lone siomai triumphed over Dizon the Devourer?'

'Nat.'

'Has something bested the record of Three Chicken Inasals in One Meal?' I power through. 'Stop the presses! Hide yo kids, hide yo wives! This moment shall go down in history as the day that—'

Lena swings her backpack at my arm with so much force that I yelp in mid-laugh. 'That was *one* time, and I hadn't eaten all day, and you starving me to death by playing all those campaigns wasn't helping!' She pouts at me, and I hold back the urge to kiss her right then. 'I was trying to be nice—which probably isn't in your vocabulary—but if you hate this siomai so much, I'll just eat it and get it over with.'

'No, I want it, mine wasn't enough—'

'Too late. You've lost your last siomai privileges—'

'It's mine—'

'No, it's not—'

'Gimme it—'

'Nat!'

'Lena!'

She poises to poke the last siomai with her toothpick, and I swipe to grab the whole tray from her. She wiggles the tray out of my reach, laughing hysterically now, and we both engage in a mad dance to fight for the last siomai. Somehow, in the middle of all the giggling and the angling and the shoving, Lena ends up pinned against the wall of the corner we're in, her gazing up at me and my hands on the wall on either side of her head.

We're both panting and giggling until the laughter grows faint on her face, and she's looking up at me and I'm looking down at her and we're so close. *We're so close.* The heat of our breaths steams the tiny space between us, and with her hair down, her soft strands rest easy on her collarbone, exposed by her top that shows off her bare shoulders.

Why Lena picked this exact day to wear that kind of neckline is a mystery to me, but it's doing its job way too well. She feels so small like this, pinned between my body and the wall, and I feel like if I took her in my arms right now, she'd fit right against me perfectly. Her soft pants and the rise and fall of her chest and the curve of her neck and my whole body aches to touch her, to hold her, to feel her skin on my lips and to hear her sigh my name.

My eyes flicker down to her lips, slightly open, almost waiting. But this is Lena and am I crazy and why am I staring at her lips, so I look back up into her eyes, and she catches me.

She catches me staring at her lips.

And the horror in her eyes tears me apart.

A group of boys whooshes past us and jeers, 'Hoy!'

I scamper a million miles away from Lena.

The boys whistle and cackle to themselves as they slink away, and everything morphs back into view, the din of the station, the passengers left and right, and the sun setting gloriously in the distance.

Lena still has that weird look in her eye, so I grab the notorious siomai and pop the whole thing into my mouth.

Break the ice, Nat. It's just siomai. No more, no less.

I spend forever chewing, and a smile dances back onto her lips. 'Cheater,' she grumbles. I use the siomai in my mouth as an excuse not to say anything.

We both step into the train a few minutes later, and Lena tries her damnedest to talk about anything but what just happened. I guess I understand.

We'll be seeing Raf again in just a few stops, and compared to that prospect, I wouldn't want to talk about me, either.

As the train chugs along from one stop to the next, I watch as the people go by with their heads down and their hearts closed, itching to move on with their day. There doesn't seem to be any space for young love here, no room for unrequited feelings and awkward dances, missed smiles and stolen moments, the anticipation of those three dots on text messages and the flutter it leaves in the chest.

Maybe Lena will always be close enough but not close enough, and we'll soon be just like these nameless faces passing each other by in stations that meld together as one day bleeds into the next. Maybe it's a childlike hope that will snuff itself out as soon as adulthood chokes the life out of it in the real world. And maybe it's naive of me to think we can ever be anything more than this.

We step off at our stop and the doors close behind us, a reminder of the fleeting childhood things I need to leave behind.

* * *

The small space in the event hall has been transformed.

Stepping under the arch of fake vines and overgrown roots feels like phasing through a portal into an enchanted land, as Function Room A disappears only to be replaced by a rainforest in the middle of the city.

The wilderness envelops us. The lights are dim enough to simulate the shade of thick trees, and every wall has been covered with fake barks and leaves, complete with stumps here and there on the ground. What was once a carpeted floor is now littered with rocks and dry earth, and even with the soft crunching under my feet, I still can't believe hotel management allowed this kind of event styling here just for this occasion.

Tala Tales Games have gone all out. There's only a small bunch of people—forty, maybe fifty tops—but the production value is top-notch. It just goes to show how important media buzz is, especially with high-profile games like *Mitolohiya*.

Judging by how everyone is acting around one another, I would say we're in the presence of a handful of staff and mostly guests, all of whom are game journalists, influencers, and streamers. This *is* a press event after all, and yes, we are underdressed, and no, we don't belong here at all.

'Nat! Lena!' Raf's powerful voice blasts through over the din of the small talk and Lena immediately lights up beside me. He marches away from the screen up front and weaves through the standing cocktail tables toward us, that political smile never leaving his face. With his coat casually draped over his shoulder like he's a billionaire CEO on break, Raf can be a poster boy for a brick, and it will still sell like hotcakes.

'Perfect timing! The presentation's just about to start.' He leads us to an empty cocktail table. 'I might have to disappear every so often, but please, enjoy yourselves. Grab some goodie bags over there by that dude in an Engkanto hoodie. And try the tiny bread thing with the cheese on top—it's divine.'

Lena and I barely get the chance to reply before he's off, shaking hands with another group of people like he's running for office.

'He did say he'd be busy tonight.' Lena chuckles at the direction Raf disappeared in. 'This place is something, huh?'

'Yeah. Something.' A few YouTubers are snapping away at two display shelves encased in glass to one side of the hall, taking pictures of what I can only make out as *Mitolohiya* figures and other merch. Up front beside the screen, there's another glass case that's probably taller than I am, and inside is a 1:1 scale of a cool-looking kalis—this long and wavy double-edged blade with stylized rays of the sun at the hilt—and a Filipino war shield called a kalasag.

The expansion pack is supposed to feature an additional campaign that walks players through the details of the epic brawl between Apolaki and Mayari, as they battled for supremacy over the skies in ancient times. The heavens roared. The deities wailed. Utter chaos engulfed the earth.

The kalis and the kalasag are two new weapons you can equip Apolaki with, because the developers apparently think he's not overpowered enough already.

'Well, so much for taking selfies over there,' Lena nods at the group of Twitch streamers clamouring for a good shot of the new weapons.

'Does Dizon the Devourer wanna go try some tiny "bread things with the cheese on top"?'

'Does she ever.'

We lurk by the buffet table for a while, a generous spread of exotic cocktail thingies I have never seen and will never be able to pronounce. As it turns out, the event isn't a dinner per se, as there are no seats to be found at all. The food choices are either things you dip or things you dip them in, and the whole thing almost makes me want to reach into my backpack and rip into that Superman sandwich Mom made me pack this morning.

Almost.

But I'm already out of place as it is, and even though Lena's rocking a backpack as well, she still has this elegance about her that can frankly make her fit in anywhere. I, on the other hand, am not so lucky.

Still, even as we're milling about, Lena manages to turn a few heads—but only because it's obvious they're silently judging her. I've seen this crap before, and Lena herself is no stranger to these discriminatory looks. She gets them every time she steps into gaming cons and demo booths—they take one look at her and think there's just no possible way she could be a hardcore gamer. She's probably there for someone else, probably has no idea what the heck is going on.

They're wrong, though. They always are. I personally want to eradicate that blatant toxic masculinity targeted toward the Gamer Girl.

Lena is used to it by now, which is the saddest thing ever. 'We'll turn the tide someday,' she says. 'But for now, I can get back at them by hoarding as many of these freebie stickers as I can.'

We slip back to our cocktail table after a few of those bread-things-with-cheese-on-top just as the presentation starts. A representative of the Tala Tales Games development team introduces the new campaign up front, followed by a teaser in-game cinematic that lasts for just thirty seconds. All the guests are fixated on the screen in rapt attention, while Raf is standing at a different table with a bunch of other foreign voice actors I vaguely recognize.

After the presentation, they open up the floor for questions from the media, and the podcasters and influencers fire away.

I lean close to Lena and whisper. 'Betcha you're wishing you didn't give me the last siomai, huh.'

She plucks a breadcrumb from the cocktail table and hurls it in my direction.

When the whole thing is over, the developers set up a few laptops and invite all guests to get exclusive initial access to the first few minutes of the campaign, and as much as we're both dying to try it out, the actual press from this press event obviously get first dibs.

I'm about to invite Lena to slip out of the hall with me when Raf waves us over to the demo area, where the crowd looks like it's ready to balloon up and explode. Lena shakes her palms politely in front of her to refuse, but Raf mouths 'come on' with an insistent grin on his face.

'Go ahead,' I tell Lena. 'Just need the bathroom for a bit.'

'Come find me right after,' she says, then makes her way over to where Raf is waiting.

Everything vacuums to silence the moment I slip out of the hall. There's barely anyone else on this side of the hotel wing, and as I follow the signs to the restrooms, I ask myself why I left Lena alone with Raf to experience one of the coolest things in the world. Do I feel *that* hopeless against his glistening charm that I just . . . gave up altogether?

I lean against the fancy sink and catch my reflection in the mirror, and yep—nothing special there.

One of the coolest things Josh and I learned (and retained) from Biology class was this certain horned lizard that, when push comes to shove, can shoot a nasty stream of blood from its eyes and squirt it right into its predator's disgusted face. I remember thinking how ultra-badass that was, to be so aggressively ready to defend yourself that you use your own blood as a weapon.

I'm no horned lizard. Up against this gargantuan Big Boss in my life right now, I've got no final defence mechanisms left.

I shove my hands in my pockets and make my way back to the hall when Lena emerges just as I'm about to head back in.

'Hey.'

'Hey.' I stop mid-stride. 'How was it?'

'Divine. I wish I could keep playing, but there was a line behind me, so.' Lena tilts her head to one side, and we stand there staring at each other.

I bury my hands even deeper into my pockets. Now that we are alone again without the weight of the crowd pressing down on us, I struggle to find the right words to say. 'Um. You look nice today, by the way.'

She smiles. 'Thanks. You don't look too bad yourself.'

'In an old T-shirt?'

'It's a V-neck. I like it when you wear those.' She points at my chest. 'Gives me a peek at the goods.'

I burn up. 'Umm. What?'

'I have a thing for collarbones,' she says casually, tugs at both of her backpack straps, and nods. 'Let's go home.'

'O-okay.'

Lena doesn't say much the whole train ride. Every now and then, I sneak a sideways glance at her and catch her rubbing her eyebrows like she's trying to ward off a bad headache. I open my mouth to speak, but realize she will probably just withdraw from the conversation if I start talking, and my mouth promptly shuts close.

Right before our last stop, Lena breaks the silence. 'Thanks for everything today.'

'I didn't do much.'

'You didn't,' she chortles, her voice soft. She then proceeds to fish something out of her backpack. 'Almost makes me wish I didn't get this for you.'

Lena hands me the small paper bag she picked up at that personalized stuff kiosk a while ago.

I shake the contents onto my open palm, and out pop two keychains in the shape of a puzzle piece, one the broken half of the other. One of them has 'WhyNotCocoNat' engraved on it while the other one says 'Relentless_Lena', and on both the puzzle pieces, it says, 'Co-ops for Life'.

It would have been the most romantic gift ever, if only I wasn't certain that Lena has no romantic feelings for me whatsoever.

Still, it kind of makes the gift I prepared for her birthday tomorrow feel anti-climactic now.

'For when we head off to college,' Lena says. 'Whole new world out there.'

I attach the prized keychain to the zipper of my backpack, and Lena does the same for her other half. My throat grows thick. 'Yeah. Thanks, Lena. This is ultra-cool.'

We step off of the train onto the looming maze of the station, the puzzle piece glinting on my bag like the beacon of hope it supposedly is. There is a pulling sensation in my gut.

Despite what the keychain says, why does it feel like Lena just gave me a token to say goodbye?

Four

In Which My Monetization
and Retention Schemes Suck

Game Concept Proposal by Nathaniel Carpio
Genre: Battle Royale/Survival Shooter
*An uber-cool decked-out avatar named NatTheNoobSlayer has all
the right cosmetics like those themed weapon skins and emotes you
only get during limited-time events. He is a total pay-to-win player,
and he is not ashamed to show it. He preps his gear in his uber-sleek
lobby and waits for the matchmaking to begin. When the countdown
starts, he flexes his virtual muscles, strikes a dance pose you can only
buy with in-game currencies from the shop, and the fun begins.*

*The initial jump is effortless. He knows exactly where to
land and exactly where the supply crates are. He skydives into the
battlefield like a boss, scopes out the ninety-eight other players in the
arena, and gets rid of them one by one with ease and in the most
creative ways possible. Then, when the kill zone gets smaller and
smaller, he stands in the middle of the street, waiting for that one
other player to show up—some loser named DaftRaf. And when he
does, our hero bombards him with all the firepower he's got.*

*DaftRaf scurries behind an abandoned building and
NatTheNoobSlayer slides across the battlefield and spots him in an
instant. He whittles down DaftRaf's Health Points until he's down
to his last, pathetic breath, and he stands over him and holds back.*

NatTheNoobSlayer wants DaftRaf to remember this moment, this last attempt for DaftRaf to grovel and beg for his life, this pitiful excuse to weasel his way out of his own demise at the foot of the obviously superior player.

'Why are you doing this?' DaftRaf slobbers, a measly mess on the ground. 'What have I ever done to you?'

At this, NatTheNoobSlayer bends down to give DaftRaf a closer look at his own doom. 'Because you stole my Lena away from me, you pompous prick. And now you die.'

NatTheNoobSlayer shoots him in the head. No mercy, no regrets.

The 'Winner, Winner Chicken Dinner' screen flashes on his screen, because he's just that cool, because he's just that awesome. Then he logs off and brags about his win to the love of his life, who's been waiting for him to win that match, and then they ride off into the sunset and stuff.

The End.

Public. Static. Print. Squiggly Line.

It's another lecture day at Tala Tales Games, and unfortunately, Lena and I have been assigned to different groups.

Public. Static. Print. Squiggly Line.

So, our moderator today is scribbling random words on a whiteboard up front, while a handful of us eager beavers in the programme are staring blankly and trying our damnedest to pretend we understand a single thing. I tried to distract myself by writing down a draft of my game concept proposal that I'm supposed to submit after this whole programme, but it kinda sucks, so I tore off everything I scribbled and decided I'll start over some other day.

Right now, though, my eyes keep drifting through the glass walls of the conference room to the other room beside us, where a bunch of people are huddled together and hunched over a single laptop, their clothes all wrinkled and their hair in complete disarray. They look like they're pulling an all-nighter of some sort, and for some odd reason, I kind of want to know what the fuss is all about.

'Hello, world!'

Our bubbly mod, a twenty-something guy in a bright neon orange hoodie with a Tala Tales Games button pin on his chest, puts the cap back on his marker and beams at us. He's sporting a lanyard that says 'Girl Gamers Rock' for his company ID, which, for some bizarre reason, makes me imagine he's got a funky sister at home whose lanyard he accidentally grabbed in a hurry to get to work today. And he's rocking the lanyard too, dishing out programming wisdom like it's nobody's business, like he's got the coolest job in the world.

I get a quick, random desire to be like him someday.

'So, this might look like random words to you—some of you might even think they're not words at all—but every programmer has to go through this rite of passage if you're serious about game dev. It's an initiation!' He claps his hands together with such enthusiasm that the kid beside me jolts awake. 'You'll use different languages depending on what you want to accomplish—there's Java, Python, Swift, and other what-have-yous—but they can all make this simple "Hello World" program like *that*.'

He snaps his fingers for effect, then writes another code on the board, flashing us his pearly whites afterward. 'Now, I've written up this simple code over here for ya in Python, but you can try it out at home in Java and see for yourself! Bonus points for whoever tries it out successfully, yeah?'

At this, a bunch of us start jotting down the lines of code in our notebooks, so I begrudgingly do the same. While I do find all of this pretty cool, I just can't concentrate on any of it right now, when my mind keeps wandering to Diwatas and forest fairies and a particular YouTuber's punchable face.

'Alright, so.' Orange Hoodie Dude taps his smartwatch. 'We've still got a few more minutes before I need to lead you out of here and onto the pantry, so I'll go ahead and start on the next topic. I know, I know—you're all eager to get your hands on the unlimited snacks, but this won't be long.'

He then starts talking about the mobile game industry and how monetization and retention schemes work to rake in new players and keep them there, because if all you ever have is a novel idea, players will eventually lose interest and move on to the next free-to-play thing. One kid actually groans, because Orange Hoodie Dude was not kidding about the pantry—they have an all-you-can-eat buffet table here but for the unhealthiest snacks Mom would probably ban me from. It's like an open invitation to make bad decisions as fuel for creative coding—the more sinful the snack, the more brilliant the idea.

Our mod moves on to explain pay-to-win schemes and this thing called the 'gacha' system, where you roll for the most powerful characters in the game but have to pay a premium to get the cool 5-star ones. Everything I'm learning from this programme is fascinating—I mean, it certainly beats the science summer camp thingy I went to in junior year, where we basically just toured some university's bio lab and watched someone demonstrate how to extract fingerprints off a glass (okay, so that was pretty cool). But there was also this lab where we watched someone dissect a cat, so, no, thanks.

Here though, I'm learning a few things I'd like to know more about, if I do nab that scholarship—and I honestly want to. With Mom losing her job and the internet cafe the only thing keeping us afloat these days, the scholarship could not come at a better time. Which is why it's probably best if I got my head out of this whole Lena headspace, because obsessing over my mission to defeat the Big Boss Raf isn't doing my future in the academe any favours. Plus, just being good at *Mitolohiya* probably isn't the best way to get picked.

I know it's what I have to do, so why is it still so damn hard to do it?

I rub my temples just as Orange Hoodie Dude lets us off the hook, and all in good time, too.

A bucket of nachos drowning in an unholy amount of cheese is exactly what I need right now.

* * *

'Apolaki. Diwata Clan.' I click on a link on the *Mitolohiya* Wiki. 'Hero class. Headstrong, independent. Can kick anyone's ass solo.'

Josh pops his gum beside me in Carpio Diem, the two of us chilling before I have to leave and pick up Lena. 'Uh-huh.'

'You can only choose either Apolaki or Mayari in your line-up, though. The developers stayed true to the beef.'

'Beef?'

'Yeah. You know. The myth? Apolaki and Mayari fought over the skies until he accidentally blinded one of her eyes in the scuffle. Now, the two siblings share the heavens in peace— Apolaki would rule the day with his ruthless blaze while gentle Mayari would rule the night with her one eye.'

'Ah.'

'So that's what the Diwata Clan is all about.' I type in *Rafael Antonio game strategy* on Google's search bar. 'Like, it relies too heavily on its heroes. You level up their skills and you're unstoppable. It's all about being able to customize skills and adapt based on whom you're fighting. Lena's good at that kind of thing.'

'Okay.'

'The Aswang Clan—they're like, super feral. It's all about speed, brute force, and strength in numbers. There's no one single unit that can storm a base or win a battle. There's not enough room for flexibility when it comes to strategy, but that just means they're reliable. Which is what I like about them.'

'Which also means you're stiff and unable to switch things up when life calls for it.' Josh lets out a huge, totally rude yawn. 'And this is why I always regret it when I ask you about *Mitolohiya*.'

'Hey, you *wanted* me to distract you. This is all on you.' I straighten up in my computer seat. 'Also, isn't it supposed to be date night later for you too? What are you doing nerding out with me?'

'Bea cancelled date night for some reason. I didn't ask.' Josh yawns again. 'But do go on. You talking about the mechanics of this game I don't understand might help get my mind off things.'

'Suit yourself.' I shrug. 'Okay, so. The third tribe is the Engkanto Clan, which focuses on ranged spell-casters. It's considered the hardest tribe to master for newbie *Mitolohiya* fans, but for experienced players, it can be the strongest tribe out of all three. They're virtually unstoppable toward end game.'

'Sure.'

'I'm sticking to my handy-dandy Aswang Clan, though. The Duwende are miners, so you gotta rely on them to farm minerals and resources for building your base. The Sigbin are pretty squishy with low health, but they're fast and cloaked, so they get the job done. They can go ahead and scout the whole battle map for you so you can get a better idea of the terrain you're playing on, and maybe even sneak a peek at what the enemy's bases are doing.'

'Right.'

'The Kapre and the Tikbalang are these huge sentinels on steroids, so these siege units are super effective when guarding your base. When it comes to main offensive units, my personal favourite is the Manananggal. They can melee the hell out of enemy ground units, but the best part is when you upgrade their flying skill, which is where they make the most damage to air units. With a properly upgraded Manananggal attack force, you can wipe anything out.'

'Great.'

'And I doubt you're still with me so I'm just gonna go ahead and shut up now.' I close the browser with the Wiki on it and switch back to the task at hand before Josh's *Mitolohiya* crash course.

'My eyes haven't glazed over just yet.' Josh chuckles. 'Besides, you don't have to do that, you know.' He pops his gum again and promptly licks the remnants of destruction off his lips. I never understood the thing—aren't you basically just re-chewing your own mouth filth?

I shake my head. 'It's no big deal. Besides, who *wouldn't* want to spend a good chunk of every workday setting wallpapers on thirty desktops?'

He chews on the gooey mess again and grins. 'Whatever. I appreciate it, man.'

'Like I said. No big deal.'

I work my magic on the settings of the next computer, then lean back to admire my handiwork. Now, all thirty units in Carpio Diem have bulk_smash's custom wallpaper on the home screen, his screensaver on the idle ones, and the link to his YouTube channel on every browser homepage. Sure, customers can always change the customization settings whenever, but I don't mind the painstaking task of resetting everything when they leave.

The great bulk_smash deserves all the promotional tactics in the world, and it's the least I can do.

'Well, isn't that something.' Josh scans the computers and lets out a low whistle. 'You *are* desperate for something to get your mind off your humiliating defeat, aren't you?'

'Gee, thanks.' I roll my eyes. 'This is purely for bulk_smash's benefit. Any welcome side-effects of having to do this every day is purely coincidental.'

'Right.' Josh sighs. 'Refresh my poor old memory—why are you so set on Lena, anyway?'

'Not this again.'

'I mean it. She's a nice person and all, and a great friend to you, I bet—but I just don't think she's the right one for you, you know?'

'Why? Because pretty isn't good enough for me? Smart? Cool? Talented?'

'Because ever since that day you decided you're head over heels in love with her—'

'I didn't just *decide*—'

'—you've been looking at her with rose-coloured glasses, man. All you ever see are the good things, like you're obsessed with this idea of her—that can't be healthy.'

'I'm *not* obsessed. I just—I mean—' I tug at my shirt. 'Whose side are you on, anyway?'

'Yours, man. Always. I'm just saying.'

'Nat! How's our sales report going?' Dad barges into the shop, done with giving the front steps a quick sweep. He blinks his confusion at the two of us apparently in the middle of something, then immediately recovers. 'Josh! Such an honour for our tiny shop to be graced by your presence.'

'Anything for you, Mr C.' Josh grins and walks up to my father, all previous conversations forgotten. 'How's the missus?'

'Fit as a fiddle. You know how she is.' Dad waves his hand. 'Ever since people heard about her employer closing shop, all everyone ever wants to know is how she's doing. What about me, though? I have feelings too!'

Josh laughs as Dad clutches at his chest to mock-lament his fate, and I shake my head. Carpio Diem isn't the most hopping place to be, especially with the dawn of home Wi-Fi packages and the rise of mobile gaming. Kids these days aren't scrambling to use a computer in public when they have their smartphones to pretty much do anything, so despite how my parents want to keep up appearances, I know our financial status isn't going to last.

It's only a matter of time before Dad declares he needs to get two jobs, especially if Mom can't find a new one.

My eyes inevitably travel to Unit 19, the same evil desktop Raf used to 'pwn' me at my own game.

With so many things hanging on the scholarship at Tala Tales Games, I can't help but wonder if Josh is actually on to something.

Five

In Which My Trusty Manananggal Solves My Love Problems for Me

Average build, average height, paler and with a worse posture than the average eighteen-year-old kid from my school. Eyes as dull as black can be, but Mom tells me that at the right angle, and if the lighting is just right, there's a little hint of brown in there somewhere.

That's it. I've never felt like there's anything gush-worthy about how I look, but today, I'm in a crisp white polo shirt and a nice pair of pants, hoping against hope I'll stand out enough for Lena to look twice.

But against a twenty-four-year-old voice-acting prodigy, I'm not so sure.

I take a deep breath, shake off the nerves from my hands, and ring the doorbell.

A woman in a black pantsuit answers the door with a smile, her straight bob reminding me of Black Widow in that Captain America movie.

'Hey, Nat,' Amihan Dizon eyes me up and down and winks. 'Looking sharp.'

'Thanks, *Ate* Ami.' I flush. 'Um. Is Lena ready to go?'

'Just about. I'd invite you in but it's a pigsty in here right now. Pipe under the kitchen sink gave way just as I was about to leave for work. Now the whole house smells like a sewer.' She calls out behind her with audible stress. 'Pa! Nat's here!'

I peer over her shoulder and spot Lena's father slouching in the small living room, messy beard and sunken eyes with a bottle of beer in his hand. He shifts his head away from the TV just for a second, blinks at me, nods his recognition, then returns to his programme.

'Same old, same old,' *Ate* Ami clucks her tongue, just as Lena bounds down the wooden stairs and marches right up to the doorway.

Her hair is down. Soft, bouncy curls rest easily on her shoulders, the shorter, uneven strands in front tucked behind one ear. I never know what they're called, but she's wearing one of those effortless, flowy dresses that end just below her knees, casual and chill and brighter than the sun. The mismatched laces on her Chucks and the sideways pursed lips and Lena is Lena, gorgeous and smiling and breaking my heart.

'There she is! Happy birthday, Little Lena.' *Ate* Ami swipes at Lena's nose just as she ducks away. 'Be home by twelve.'

'*Aaa-te.*' Lena tugs at her earphones and dangles them down her shoulders. 'You can't be serious!'

'I mean it.' *Ate* Ami eyeballs me with a teasing smirk. 'She is eighteen, but I still have the one copy of the house key. Until I get this thing duplicated, you guys come home when I want you to.'

'Yeah, yeah.' Lena groans and seizes my arm. 'Let's go, Nat.'

'Uh, bye, *Ate* Ami.' I raise my hand all awkward at her grinning face as Lena drags me away. We hurry to the sidewalk where the cab I booked is waiting for us, and the moment we pull away from the kerb, Lena bounces in her seat.

'So. Where are you taking me on this fine day?'

'You'll see.' I smile at her, rubbing my sweaty palms on my pants as discreetly as possible. *Relax, Nat. It's just like any other day. It's just Lena.*

Radiant, beautiful, birthday girl Lena.

She shrugs then, casually launching into a conversation about random topics ranging from the busted kitchen pipe to her phone's storage space. Raf's name comes up a few times, but I'm too focused on what I need to do to pull off this afternoon perfectly that it doesn't even bother me.

When we get off in front of a fancy hotel with classy chandeliers and high ceilings, Lena's face pales.

'Uh, Nat? You sure we're in the right place?' She gapes at the towering building.

'Just follow my lead.' I raise my chin and hope it's reassuring enough, because my feigned confidence can only go so far. We step through the heavy glass doors and cross the lobby to the receptionist, who greets us with a warm smile.

'Good afternoon, ma'am, sir,' she says. 'How may I help you today?'

'Hi.' I smile back. 'We were just wondering how to get to the rooftop bar?'

'Oh, of course.' She gestures toward the elevators lined up to one side. 'Just press the Sky Deck button and the elevator should take you right up to the penthouse.'

'Great.' I ignore the pulse in my throat. 'Thanks so much.'

'You're very welcome,' she replies with a little wave.

The moment the elevator doors close and the fancy background music comes on, Lena chuckles. 'What shenanigans are you up to, kind sir? Not a sneaky Aswang tactic to lure the innocent Diwata to her untimely demise, I hope?'

'Just some minor mischief. No skill points allotted to the Backstab skill whatsoever.' I puff up my chest in what I hope is a confident stance. 'A special treat for the lady's special day.'

The elevator opens right into the hotel's rooftop, an open deck with a private pool surrounded by lounge chairs and woven benches. To one side is a small chill-out bar where some lo-fi music is playing. A few hotel guests are hanging about, wisps of conversation drifting in and out of focus, like there's an invisible threshold when it comes to the general volume around here over the tinkling of the silverware.

I approach the booth where fresh towels are stacked on the shelves and greet the attendant. 'Hiya. Do we need to surrender our room key here?'

'Oh, no need for that, sir!' The attendant is caught off-guard. 'Please, go ahead and enjoy the amenities. Will you be needing some towels?'

'No, that's okay.' I flash him a polite smile. 'We'll just hang out and relax for a bit, if that's alright.'

'Of course, sir. How about some complimentary drinks?'

'Just some shakes, please, if it's not too much to ask?'

'Right away, sir!'

I grin my thanks at the attendant, and we find a spot on one of the lounge chairs around the pool with a spectacular view overlooking the city. There's a small menu propped up on the side table, and I pick it up.

'Okay, so, now we actually have to order something.'

Lena throws me a look of awe. 'I'm impressed. Who would have thought Nathaniel Carpio had a fancy side? Consider me fancied.'

'The afternoon's just begun.' I drag a hand through my hair. 'We order a regular overpriced pasta, and they'll serve us unlimited gourmet bread with those sophisticated dips.'

Lena giggles. When the kind attendant arrives with our meal a few minutes later, I ask for the Wi-Fi password.

I wave my phone at Lena. 'Guild event in half an hour.'

'You *have* thought of everything, haven't you?'

'I try.'

She giggles again and I take that desperate, fleeting moment to capture everything about her, quiet and loud at the same time.

We spend the next few hours just sitting there, munching on our snacks and chatting about random things and watching the sun go down, miraculous and melancholy across the sky. Lena hums random soundtracks for some of the guests that come and go, toasting to the ultra-buff guy in Speedos and the woman with an odd kind of breaststroke. At one point, a beachside beat comes on and Lena closes her eyes and sways to the music. All I can do is watch, every tilt of her head mesmerizing, every sway of her hips a stab in my side.

And just like that, night falls, and the city comes alive below us, the lights on the buildings and the cars speeding along the streets. Low-hanging fairy lights blink into view across the roof deck, tea candles flicker on the floor, and soft music weaves through the evening breeze.

'This is just like you, Nat.'

'What do you mean?'

'Just . . . you. Being nice to everyone. I mean, we're a couple of freeloaders here but you didn't muscle your way through or anything. You didn't wow anyone with pretentious arrogance or elbow anyone out of your way,' she says. 'You were just nice and polite and a hundred percent Nathaniel, and now we're here.'

I scratch my throat and go red. 'Dad taught me all of this stuff for today. Otherwise, I would have absolutely no idea what to do. I didn't even know this place existed.'

'You didn't have to do all this, you know. We could've just hung out at the grillery, and I'd be just as happy.' She hugs herself, almost like she's trying to contain a feeling. 'Still. It's a nice change of pace.'

'I figured you could people-watch a different crowd here.'

'Well, there is that.' She rocks back and forth in her seat. 'The vibe is different. Every scene is a track, and every track is an art piece, you know? And there's always emotion in there, somewhere, somehow. I just have to figure out how it makes me feel, how it makes other people feel, and enhance that feeling.' She shuffles her feet and cringes. 'Sorry. Nerd talk.'

'Hey—it's me you're talking to. I'm as much of a nerd as anyone will ever be.'

'That I agree with.' She lurches sideways to pinch my arm and I mock-dodge her attacks, the two of us doing that manic dance again. She shoves me, her face flushed, and settles for slapping my forearm instead.

'It's so easy, talking to you like this. I mean, even if you have no idea what I'm talking about.' Her laughter fades and she shifts her position, and suddenly we're shoulder to shoulder, her skin sending both fire and ice through my body at the same time. 'I wish I could talk to *Ate* Ami like this too. You know, without her judging me or anything.'

'She's not going to judge you, Lena. What does that even mean?' I clear my throat and focus on the topic at hand. '*Ate* Ami's the most awesome-sauce sister in the world.'

'I don't know, Nat. It's just that sometimes I feel like if I talked to people about my passions and stuff, I'd—' Lena stops short, her face contorting into an expression I can't read.

'What is it?'

'It's just . . . I just wish things were easier.' She rubs a spot on her neck, and when her hand drops down beside mine, my throat dries.

'Yeah.' I whisper. 'I wish things were easier too.'

She tosses me a sad smile. 'You're lucky though, with Tito and Tita. With a support system like that, the future doesn't seem so scary. There's not much reason to be afraid, you know?'

Her sad smile carves its way into my chest, and I have never felt more terrified in my entire life. 'It's . . . not that simple.'

'Right, sorry. Parents, am I right? Can't live with them, can't live without them.'

She turns away and the moment is gone, Lena taking my fear along with her.

I guess I understand what she means. Lena never spent time with her mother. She left when Lena was way too young, forcing her older sister Ami, who's twelve years her senior, to take their mother's place. Not long after that, Lena's father developed a formula for the car company he was working for at the time, a way for vehicles to utilize an auto-brake function for the ultimate safety and convenience.

It failed. Of the countless scenarios Lena's father tested, he overlooked one small mistake that doomed the whole project. His brilliant mind then failed along with the auto-brake failure, his career ruined, and his conscience forever tainted with the cost of an innocent person's life. He withdrew into himself, wasting away in their living room couch day after day, with a bottle in one hand and a fistful of guilt in the other.

He was never mean to his two girls, never hurt them, never laid a hand on them. But he just lost his own will to live, and *Ate* Ami has been the sole breadwinner of their little family since then.

She's doing well as the VP for Finance at this multinational IT company, so the Dizons aren't having too much trouble scraping by. But Lena always feels like she's a huge burden on her sister, blaming herself for not being able to contribute to their finances sooner.

'So . . . did Mr Dizon like the *Lord of the Rings* trilogy? You mentioned he enjoyed *Dragonheart* before, so I figured he'd enjoy all the high fantasy.'

'Oh. Yeah.' Lena looks confused for a bit. 'He did. Marathoned the whole thing, in fact.'

'That's awesome. I still have a bunch of other recos in my room. I'll be sure to send them over.'

Lena smiles a distracted smile at me. 'That's sweet, Nat. He's going to love them, I'm sure. Thank you.'

'Hey, I'm happy to share what I have with a fellow movie buff.' I grin at her and she grins back, but there's a hint of wetness pooling along the corners of her eyes, so I turn away.

'Umm. So. Whatever this is about your future, it's why we have the scholarship, right?' I try to lighten the mood. 'Look out, Tala Tales Games. Relentless_Lena's gonna blow everyone away.'

Her eyes are vacant now, and her throat makes an odd noise. 'Yeah . . .' Her eyes drop. 'The scholarship.'

Despite my best efforts, I have somehow managed to ruin this night.

And then I remember my saving grace.

'Speaking of Tala Tales Games. I almost forgot.' I fumble into my pocket and hand her a small velvet pouch with the game developer's logo on it. 'Happy birthday.'

I watch as Lena gingerly tugs on the drawstring, and an engraved coin-like piece falls onto her open palm. A moment of realization later and her eyes widen.

'You didn't.'

I'm pretty sure there's a sheen of sweat glistening on my whole face by now, but I still hope Lena can't see how much I'm blushing. 'The other half of Bathala's amulet. Just . . . a small throwback to when we first met.'

'But this is worth so much money, Nat,' she lets out a soft gasp. 'How did you . . .?'

'I've . . . been saving up for it for a while. I was going to give it to you as a graduation gift, but I hadn't saved up enough by the time our graduation rites came along.' I shove my hands into my pockets. 'I had to get creative. I eventually opened up a new *Mitolohiya* account and levelled up the hero skills enough until the account got sold at a good price.'

'Nat . . .'

Lena's voice trembles as much as my heart does, so I have to look down before my face betrays how I feel.

To my surprise, she hands me her phone. I look back up at her.

'Take a picture, will you?' She smiles and dangles the half-amulet near her face. The moment I lift her phone, my hands shake.

Looking at Lena at the centre of the shot, I unravel. Her head is tilted to one side against the backdrop of stars littered across the infinite darkness behind her.

Just when I think I can't fall harder and deeper for my best friend, I do.

'Got it?'

I nod, and she shifts her position and sits right beside me on the lounge chair, leaning her body as close to mine as possible. 'Now a selfie, okay?'

Lena's so close I can smell her shampoo. 'Okay.'

I hold out her phone in front of us and try to smile at the camera like my whole body isn't hyperventilating.

'Okay, 1, 2, 3—'

And then, right as I tap on the button to take the photo, Lena turns and kisses me on the cheek. The transparent expression on my face is immortalized in that photo forever.

'Thanks, Nat,' she whispers in my ear, 'for the best birthday ever.'

Stage Two: Level Up

Six

In Which Online Trophies
Mean Squat on Easy Mode

What motivates you? By Nathaniel Carpio
Love. Love is what motivates me. I know that sounds cheesy, but
it's true. Love makes the world go round and all that, doesn't it? To
do your very best for her. To want to excel in everything. To make
her happy and drive all her sadness away.

Love is what motivates me to wake up in the morning. To face
the future's uncertainty. To know that things changing can be scary
but to be okay with it, because if she's going to be in my future, how
bad can it be?

There is no fear in love, after all, right?

'This is absolute crap.' I spam the 'Delete' key and erase every word. The networking night is coming up in a few days, which means this stupid essay plus my game concept proposal are going to be due shortly after. Even though I haven't seen Lena in three days since our little birthday rendezvous, I haven't stopped thinking about her. Every scene from that night replays in my mind in agonizing detail over and over again, every waking hour of the day.

Which is why every time I try to start writing this horrific thing, it always ends up being about Lena. After the nth draft, I still haven't made any progress.

The morning after the most awkward, most beautiful kiss on my cheek, Lena started texting me again like she normally does, making it painfully obvious that the kiss meant nothing. She was probably just grateful for the gift and had a nice night. It was just a 'thank you'. Just a little token of her appreciation. Just a quick peck on the cheek of a guy she's in a platonic relationship with. That's all there is to it.

Despite the facts, I've successfully spent three sleepless nights obsessing over it.

Still, whatever it was, I'm pretty sure it's landed me on a spot way closer to her heart now, leaving airhead Rafael Antonio behind in the dust.

Speaking of . . .

My phone screen lights up with Lena's text message, telling me she's on her way to the grillery. I speed out my room into the hallway and dash down the stairs into the shop.

Two guys are huddled in a corner working on a thesis or something, and Dad's lazing behind the counter, scrolling through his phone. 'Heading out for lunch—do you want anything, Dad?' I call out as I pass him by, and he throws me an absent-minded wave without looking at me.

There is a slight drizzle outside, the bizarre, freakish kind that happens every once in a while despite the high heat of summer. A sun shower, I think it's called, and Mom always said that when it happens, a *tikbalang* is being wed or something like that. Given my exposure to Philippine mythology being solely limited to *Mitolohiya* characters, it's just hard to imagine that the big melee brute unit from the Aswang Clan is capable of getting married.

I pull down my cap a little lower on my head and tuck my hands into my pockets, keeping up a slightly quicker pace than usual. The nameless sidewalk grillery isn't too far from our house, so I should still get there ahead of Lena.

I'm right. I shake off some of the rainwater once I'm under the shelter of the small roof and pick our seats right next to the exhaust. Then, the strangest thing happens.

As I stare at the empty bar stool beside me, I'm suddenly overcome by this heavy, overwhelming sadness in my chest, alone in the grillery with no one else around. Under the quiet rain, the sidewalk is empty, just the light pitter-patter on the aluminium roof and the tentative ripples on the puddles on the floor. The ghost of Lena's smile fades in and out in my mind's eye, fleeting and elusive, followed by a constricting loneliness I can't explain.

I clutch myself.

As I sit there wallowing in a sudden downpour of loss, Lena appears through the haze, jogging toward me with the biggest smile on her face. Stray strands of her wet hair cling to the sides of her face, her damp, oversized shirt revealing one pink bra strap on her shoulder underneath. She splashes through and settles into the seat beside me.

'Raf took me to the recording studio today,' she says, breathless and beaming.

And all the euphoria of seeing Lena again after three whole days crumbles. 'What?'

'Behind the scenes. Where he records his voiceovers. He took me on a sorta backstage pass, and I got to see all the sound mixing at work,' Lena goes on, the exhilaration clear as day in her greyish eyes. 'It was the most amazing thing ever.'

'That's great, Lena.' I force a smile. 'What was he recording?'

'Expansion pack.' Lena bites her lip in glee. 'Everyone's taking a quick lunch break right now, but I'll head back there again in a while.'

'All afternoon?' There's a bitter tang in my mouth. 'We have those extra training sessions together, remember? You know, for the tournament.'

'Oh. Right.' Lena's face falls. 'I just . . . I'll call to cancel.'

'No, no, don't. It's . . . not every day you get to see the sound stage at work. You should go.'

Lena bites her lip. 'Are you sure? God, I feel terrible.'

'I'll be fine. I promise.' My thoughts and my feelings collide in a violent act of protest. 'If you feel that bad about it, just let me win at least one game and we'll call it even.'

She bites her lip again, then her eyes light up. 'Why don't you come with me?'

'What?'

'Come with! To the sound stage!' Lena snaps her fingers. 'You'll get to experience all the magic coming alive with me. I'm sure it's fine.'

'Oh. I don't think I . . .' My words trail off, because with the way Lena's beaming at me, there's just no way I can refuse.

The six-peso coin flickers in my memory.

'Umm. Okay. Sure.'

'Awesome! Thanks, Nat. This is a big deal for me,' Lena says. 'I honestly think you'll ace the competition even without my help.'

'Nobody's better than Relentless_Lena.' There's a pesky drop of rainwater lingering on her right cheek, and I fight the urge to brush it away. 'How's your essay coming along?'

Lena hesitates. 'It's . . . coming along.'

'I know, right? I haven't started, either.' I wave my hand, but there is a tight expression on Lena's face I can't understand. 'What?'

She blinks a few times. 'It's nothing.' She swivels her bar stool and skims the grimy menu on the wall behind the counter. 'So, what'll it be? The usual? We have to be quick, though—we need to head back in a bit.'

I watch as Lena bites her lip in concentration at the menu, and that crushing sadness from a while back suddenly makes complete sense.

* * *

'Burn, for the wrath of the Sun bears down on you this day.'

Raf repeats his line for the nth time this afternoon, as we're all gathered on the other side of the recording booth, observing his performance. He's been nailing line after line for this new expansion pack they're releasing soon, and even though he's just a regular guy with his white shirt and the tailored navy blazer and the snug jeans, he really does exude all the nobility of the Sun God.

Lena is over by another corner doing technical stuff with the sound mixers, so I'm stuck here staring at Raf delivering Oscar-worthy performances with every take.

When everyone decides to take a break, he approaches me with that glowing, satisfied smile. I know exactly how pleased he is with himself, and if I had half the confidence oozing from him right now, I could conquer the world.

'Nat! So glad you can join us this afternoon.' He offers me a solid handshake, firm and reassuring. 'Enjoying yourself, I hope?'

'Yeah,' I say in spite of myself. 'Thanks for the invite. This is pretty cool.'

'Pretty cool, indeed.' He hooks his thumbs into his belt loops, his legs wide. 'New maps, new skins, the works. The expansion pack's going to be amazing.'

'It already is to me, and it's not even out yet.' Lena zips up to us, electric sparks of exhilaration exploding from all around her. 'I can't believe I'm here!'

Raf chuckles in my general direction, and I can't, for the life of me, understand why that simple gesture looks so charming on him. 'I wasn't expecting you'd come. Didn't you say your sister wanted you to run some errands for her today?'

'I told her I had to study for some programming stuff. Don't worry about it,' Lena shrugs, and I grit my teeth.

She's lying to *Ate* Ami now? How many times has she used the scholarship as an excuse just so she can sneak out and hang out with Raf? Is this how she wants to build her future career?

Raf tilts his head, puffs out his chest, and smiles at a point somewhere behind my left ear. 'Oh hey, the refreshments are here.'

An assistant brings sealed cups of milk tea for the whole staff, and everyone thanks Raf while he insists that everyone help themselves. He offers an ice-cold cup to Lena. 'I wasn't sure what kind you wanted, so I just ordered the most basic one. I hope that's okay.'

No, it's not okay, because I know exactly the kind of milk tea Lena likes—the roasted tea variant, with creamy milk foam, no sugar but with extra tapioca pearls, and no ice.

But Lena takes the milk tea from Raf, all breathless for some reason. 'Don't sweat it. I love milk tea.'

And Raf grins right back. 'Perfect.'

He offers one to me too, and as I don't want to be a jerk, I accept.

I just don't get it. I keep waiting for Raf to slip up, to tick every item in the Official Douchebag Checklist and expose him for the fraud that he is. Here is how the checklist should go:

1. He would brag about his achievements while waiting to see how others would react, then try to downplay his accomplishments with false modesty.
2. Every time someone talks about something, he would steer the topic back to himself oh-so-sneakily to dominate the conversation.

3. He would be extra animated when he knows there's an audience, complete with the booming laugh and the sense of entitlement.
4. He would praise the hard work of the whole crew and say it's a team effort, but only to remind everyone else of his own involvement in the project's success.
5. And then, he would sweep Lena off her feet and rub it in my face.

But the thing is that he's never done anything on that list, not even close. And it pisses me off.

'So, how's all the sitting in so far?' Raf asks Lena, who bursts into another luminous smile.

'It's been beyond amazing.' She rocks on her heels. 'I'm learning all these new things, and I haven't even seen everything yet. It's so magical to experience all the sound designers and audio engineers collaborating to make things work. I just hope I can do the same one day.'

'You should hear her work,' I pipe in, surprising myself. 'Lena's a genius.'

Lena flings a cold, hard look at me, her lips flat. 'No, I'm not—'

'That's a good idea,' Raf says. 'I'll try and see if I can get some of the folks together for a demo or something.'

She doesn't say anything for a while, so I speak up on her behalf.

'That's awesome, Raf. You won't regret it.'

'I know I won't.'

Lena's laughter comes with an edge, and her tone is controlled. 'Nat . . .'

'You should have more confidence in yourself, Lena.' My voice cracks. 'You're amazing.'

Lena surveys me with another shocked look on her face, only this time, it's coupled with gratitude and—maybe—a little bit of affection in there somewhere too.

That same look reminds me so much of the very first time Lena showed me her work, when we were at Carpio Diem after hours with no one else around. She brought her flash drive, did some manic pacing for a while, and plugged it in. After two minutes of radio silence from her as her trailer played out in front of us, I was floored.

It was the original trailer of the first movie we ever saw together, a rerun of an old horror film that tanked at the box office. The premise was a group of hapless teenagers playing a video game where the main antagonist came to life and murdered everyone. The video-game-villain-turned-real-person massacred anyone who has ever played the game in the most gruesome ways, and I remember thinking it was crap, but Lena spliced her own audio mix into the trailer. And everything changed.

It was supposed to be a supernatural horror flick, but the impact of a good background score can turn things around. The music ebbed and flowed like the tide, rising and falling at just the right moments, catching feelings and caging emotions and evoking weird little stirrings inside me.

The fact that Lena chose this movie as her project also told me how much she valued our time together, and there she was, baring her heart and soul to me in that piece she had never shown anyone else before. It was the first time I ever thought we had a chance.

She closed the application when it was over and sneaked a glance at me. She was patting her pockets and digging in her backpack for a non-existent thing she had lost somehow. 'Well? You hate it, don't you?'

'Damn, Lena. This trailer—it's the stuff of legends.'

'Yeah?'

'Yeah. I wish I had awesome talents like that.'

'You do have talents. You're super nice and you work super hard.'

'I said *talents*, Lena. Those things aren't skills. Besides, working hard all day doesn't get you far. I'm like that Non-Playable Character in the village who does the same thing day in and day out, never to leave town and become a hero.'

'Don't sell yourself short, Nat—you're not an NPC. And I'm not all that great, either.' She looked pleased, but she turned all red too. 'Besides, you're just saying that because you're my best friend.'

'I'm not.' I shook my head. 'I'm saying it as a guy who felt all the feels with your work. The *feels*, Lena.'

'The thing is, though, I don't see you as a guy.'

'Hey. I was, last time I checked.' I shrugged. 'At least, that's what I saw when I took a bath this morning.'

'First of all, *gross*. Second, I *mean*—' Lena nudged me. '—you're not a guy. You're Nat.'

'Ouch.'

She rolled her eyes. 'You know what I mean.' She bit her lip. 'You're *my* Nat.'

Raf pulls me back to the present with a firm clap on my back. 'Let's get going with the rest of these lines, then we can set up that meeting with the mixers. How does that sound?'

Lena doesn't need to say anything else, because that 'look' that I thought held any affection for me suddenly turned to Raf. With the way she's gazing at him like he's the answer to all of her prayers, I realize that despite the magical night Lena and I had during her birthday, it's only magical for me. It's nothing remotely close to how happy Raf has been making her lately.

Just when I think I've unlocked an achievement, the world never fails to remind me that I'm still on easy mode, and that it's a long, long way to go before I make genuine progress inside Lena's heart.

* * *

'If it makes you feel any better, Bea and I aren't doing so well right now, either.'

I lower the volume on my hundredth *Uncharted* playthrough in my room that night. Some NPC on a shipping vessel is wishing Nathan Drake well after another good haul, off to a good night's rest at the end of the day. What I would give to be that Non-Playable Character right now, his fate pretty much secure in this grand storyline. I'm pretty sure Shipping Guy doesn't have to worry about any heartbreak woes of his own.

'What do you mean?'

Josh leans back in my computer chair and shrugs. 'We kind of broke up.'

'Kind of?' I put the PlayStation controller down. 'How can you *kind of* break up with someone?'

'Well, she said she wanted to see what else is out there, now that we're about to start college. She sort of got tired of all the toys. I think she sees me as this little kid who plays with action figures all the time.' Josh shoves his hands in his pockets. 'Okay, I guess she really did break up with me, now that I think about it.'

'Jeez. What a crappy way to end it.' I sigh. 'Sorry, man.'

'Well.' He shrugs. 'It is what it is.'

'When did this happen?'

'Couple of days ago.'

'Oh.' I swallow my guilt. 'You should've told me about it.'

'It's nothing. You've got your own shiz.' He waves his hand, trying to act like it's no big deal. 'Besides, I have a handful of online buddies in this breakup forum I can rant out all my frustrations to. You should try it sometime, Nat. Maybe join one of those gaming communities on Discord or Reddit or Twitch or something.'

'I'm serious, Josh. I don't want to be one of those lousy friends who're too wrapped up in their own crap.'

'I'll be fine. You, on the other hand, I'm not so sure.' Josh gestures at the blinking cursor on my computer screen. 'Five hundred words, and all you have is your title.'

'It's a good title.'

'It's not even yours,' he says. 'Look. All you have to do is talk about what motivates you, right? You know, there's this philosopher dude who says we're all born with this inferiority complex that we strive all our lives to overcome. It's man's main motivation in life. Then there's another dude who says we're motivated by whichever stage we're fixated on during childhood, like the oral stage or the anal stage or even a stage where we're all in love with our mothers. What? I know some stuff.'

I shake my head at him. 'I'll figure it out. I just need to train for the tournament first. Without Lena's help, apparently.'

'I can't help you in that department. My hand-eye coordination is about as sharp as my boyfriend skills, which is not much, as it turns out.' Josh sighs. 'You need a video collage of why a game development company should pick you as their top scholar because you're the most awesome person in the whole wide world, you come to me.'

'You got any tips on how to upstage a hotshot voice actor from said game development company?'

He shakes his head.

'Thanks.' I sigh. 'Maybe we should start working out.'

'I'm used to gluing my butt to my chair, but sure. Like, every Marvel movie has to have a topless scene with the superhero lead, right?'

'You're thinking we could pull a Chris Pratt?'

'More Paul Rudd. We're both on the skinnier side.'

'Paul Rudd it is. I'll check out some gym memberships tomorrow. For all the good it'll do.' I look down at my super bony hands. 'Don't flake on me, man. I'll need a gym buddy for accountability.'

'I won't. And you know why we can't understand girls? It's because they've always been superior beings and our finite minds are just too limited to even try and comprehend anything that goes on in their heads.' Josh shrugs. 'Bad day for relationship noobs, huh.'

I stare at the paused cut scene on my screen, at Nate and Elena, my favourite fictional couple, hanging out in their living room playing *Crash Bandicoot* and having the time of their lives.

'Yeah,' I say. 'Really, really bad day.'

Seven

In Which I Feel Like the World is Glitching and There is No Save Point in Sight

Game Concept Proposal by Nathaniel Carpio
Genre: Turn-based RPG
A small-town boy gets whisked away into an epic adventure to save the world after a mysterious encounter with this amazing High Priestess Lena. While he doesn't know anything about her, all he knows is that he's drawn to her, and that they're meant to be together. This dangerous quest is written in the stars—it's his destiny as the Chosen One, and he must take up his sword to fight the demons and rid the world of evil to restore peace to their kingdom.

One day, the evil Raflord kidnaps the fair High Priestess and wishes to use her divine powers to unlock the gates of hell. She is the key to the Ultimate Light, the only type of magic in the world that can eliminate the darkness and wrap the whole kingdom in eternal protection. Raflord wants to corrupt her purity and steal her magic for his own dastardly deeds, and our protagonist, the brave Carpion, must stop at nothing to bring down this uber-douche.

Carpion hops from town to town to buy equipment and level up and meet colourful folks along the way to add to his party. When they stumble upon an enchanted maze in the forest one day, what they find at the heart of the woods grants Carpion unimaginable power—he unlocks a bad-ass Ultimate Skill that he can use to climb the Tower of Peril and take down the big final boss.

'But Carpion, why must you risk your life to rush into the Tower of Peril alone?' asks meek little Joshua, the steward of the royal knights. 'Tis a suicide mission, for you are but a man!'

'Nay, little Joshua,' says Carpion, staring boldly into the distance at the menacing tower of doom looming over the horizon. 'This is a quest I must take to rescue the fair High Priestess—she is lost, and now she is found. She will bring peace to this land and bathe it in her ethereal glow, and as the Chosen One, I must make this journey alone.'

And so valiant Carpion rides across the plains atop his mighty steed and charges into the Tower of Peril, wielding his Holy Sword imbued with the power of the gods, a boon bestowed upon the Chosen One, and the Chosen One alone. He slashes through the beastly fiends and unholy monstrosities guarding each floor of the seemingly endless tower, until he reaches the top floor of the evil Raflord's lair.

'Away with you, foul sorcerer!' Carpion steadies his sword and poises to strike at the super disgusting Raflord. 'Unhand the fair High Priestess and let your magicks cast fear into the kingdom no longer!'

In one final epic battle between good and evil, Carpion unleashes his Ultimate Skill and defeats Raflord and blows him to smithereens.

'Thank you, brave Carpion,' breathes the fair maiden Lena. 'Your might and mettle have saved this kingdom—have saved me.'

Carpion and the High Priestess share a kiss as a new day dawns. He left his town a boy, and now, he is coming home a warrior, ready to usher in an era of peace and live happily ever after.

No—no—no—no—

'I am Sun. I am War. And today is your reckoning.'

I hate Apolaki so damn much.

Lena pops up her head from behind my monitor in the worst kind of déjà vu. 'Ha! Another total wipe-out. C'mon, Nat. You need to do better than that if you're going to kick everyone's ass at the mixer.'

'I almost got you, you know. My Tikbalang was barely a step away from your command post.'

'The keyword is "barely", Aswang-lover.' Lena waves her arms around in the emptiness of the shop. 'All hail Relentless_Lena!'

I roll my eyes as she proceeds to make fake cheering sounds in her seat. Carpio Diem Internet Café is closed for the day, and Mom and Dad have gone ahead upstairs two hours ago. It's just Lena and me in the stuffy stillness of the shop, and we're both tied for two wins against each other.

'Alright, I need a break.' She stretches her arms over her head when she's done with her showboating. 'Want a cupcake?'

I shake my head.

'Suit yourself.'

I watch as she bites into a fluffy, strawberry-flavoured treat and gets pink icing on the tip of her nose. The box was 'just a little something' from Raf, half a dozen cupcakes just because. One of the college interns delivered it to the shop a while back, and with the way Lena was so chummy with her, it made me realize how much I don't know about what she does when she's at HQ.

Even worse than the cupcake delivery was how Lena reacted when the uber-cool assistant nodded at me and grinned at Lena. 'Who's this guy? He's cute.'

And Lena just laughed. She *laughed* and said, 'This is Nat. He won't say no to a chicken inasal date.'

'Noted.' The girl then winked at me and left. I guess I was kind of hoping Lena would at least feel a little bit of possessiveness over me, but why would she?

'I notice you've put up a couple of new *Mitolohiya* posters,' Lena says between mouthfuls of the aforementioned evil cupcakes. 'How're your parents handling the shop's newfound fame?'

'Dad's hosting a mini competition next week,' I say. 'I've never seen him this excited since that day we got the new air-conditioner.'

'I get where he's coming from,' Lena chuckles. 'When *Ate* Ami got promoted, the first thing she did was swap out our filthy unit with a brand new one. With that thing on full blast, it felt like a classic ice dungeon in there.'

'Did you get the busted kitchen pipe to work?'

'Yeah. *Ate* Ami took care of it. Wish I could've helped somehow, but you know how it is . . .' Lena slumps back in her seat, and I have to angle myself to get a good look at her. She's staring at her keyboard without saying anything, her half-eaten cupcake sitting on the table all sad and forgotten.

'Hey, Nat?'

'Hmm?'

'What do you know about sound mixing?'

'Absolutely nothing. Why?'

Lena looks up from the keyboard and right into my eyes. 'I . . . I think I want to pursue a career in it.'

'Okay, that's cool. You can do anything, Lena.'

The intensity in her eyes ignites something inside me. 'I mean, Nat, that I'm thinking of dropping out of the programme.'

My heart drops.

'I'll still show up at the networking night for sure. I'll definitely be there for you—I wouldn't want to miss your easy win.' She tries to smile. 'But I'm not going to compete anymore, Nat. I think I want a different path. I think . . . I think I want to be an audio engineer.'

What?

'I've had several conversations with *Ate* Ami about this, and she's on board. She says she wants me to follow my dreams, you know? It's not going to be a scholarship, but there are technical schools around the metro . . . maybe a community college or two . . . and I'll find myself a part-time job to help pay the fees.'

She wrings her hands together, and I have never seen her more uncomfortable in her life. 'And I know it's sudden and it's scary, but this is it, Nat. Telling a story through audio. Tinkering with all these soundtracks and music and scores. Don't they always say that if your dreams don't scare you, then that just means they're not big enough? I guess I just never gave it some serious thought until Raf came into the picture, and I'm grateful for it. It just feels like a sign, you know?'

Lena tugs at her ponytail like she's prepping for an online match. 'I want to work on something I want to do, Nat. I know I said I don't want to be like my mother, but I don't want to end up like my father, either. Reduced to the broken shell of a man because he failed and never got back up again. I'm not going to be like him. I'm going to get up again and again because I know that I love what I'm doing, failures and challenges included. I'm going to carve my own path out of my own merit. Besides, you told me that I should be more confident in myself, so here I am, declaring my own self-worth.'

She rushes through her words like the clock is ticking, and maybe it is. Her gaze bounces from place to place, but I'm at a loss for words myself, my thoughts scrambling to understand everything she just said.

She untangles her discomfort by throwing me a playful smile. 'You can't give me the silent treatment, Nat. Where are the fart jokes? The insults? The inappropriate humour? How do you feel about all this?'

She wants to know how I feel?

This is a mistake. She's making a mistake and she doesn't know what she wants and she's only saying this because stupid Rafael Antonio's been showing her all these sights, taking her to all these places, confusing her and messing with her and stealing away her future. She's an amazing sound mixer, yes, but is it worth abandoning everything over? The scholarship at Tala Tales Games is still the best option, financially and logically.

That's how I feel.

But of course, I can't tell Lena how I feel, can I?

So, I lie. 'That sounds . . . great.'

Her face lights up. 'You mean it?'

'Yeah,' my voice wavers, and I feel like reaching out to steady myself. 'It's like you said. You've always been interested in these things. And you're loads talented, Lena. Honest. You should . . . go ahead and do it.'

Lena snakes her arm through the messy wires between us and clasps my hand in hers. 'Nathaniel Carpio, I don't know what I would do without you.'

Dad picks this exact moment to saunter down the stairs. He freezes when he reaches the bottom step and sees our hands locked together, like we're sharing an intimate moment that's not breaking my heart one beat at a time.

'I, er, forgot my phone behind the register,' he barks out to no one in particular, making the situation much worse than it already is.

'I have to get home anyway.' Lena drops my hand and bolts up in her seat, slinging her backpack over her shoulder. 'Goodnight, Tito. Thanks for the free hours.'

'S-Sure. Anytime.' Dad returns her grin, and we both watch helplessly as Lena waves and slides out the door.

It happens again. Whenever Lena leaves, she yanks out a deep, painful part of me and takes it with her. Everything enters bullet time, and I can feel in maddening slow-motion the way her fingers slip away from mine. I'm left this hopeless ghost of a boy, in love and in trouble, desperately trying to prolong every moment with her, absolutely terrified, counting down the seconds I still have left.

Dad wiggles his eyebrows at me. 'Attaboy, Nat.'

* * *

'For the last time, sir, there's no virus or hidden Trojans or random spyware here.' I grit my teeth and smile through my frustration. 'It's just the mouse, see? Please don't tug on it too hard or you'll keep unplugging the USB connection.'

'This stupid mouse isn't working—it's broken and this whole crappy place is crap!' The customer throws up his hands, his nostrils flared. 'Fix your mouse. Or better yet, install better anti-virus software. My cursor keeps crashing my game! I hate this place!'

And yet, here you are, as annoying as you were yesterday. 'Of course, sir, we'll get your unit checked right away. You can transfer to Unit 29 if you'd like.'

'Of course, I'd like to transfer! Why would I want to stay in this glitching station and lose all my campaigns?' The guy flies to the unit in the other corner, and I fight the urge to shove his face right through the monitor.

He settles down in his new station and everyone turns back to whatever it was they were doing before this jerk started lamenting his terrible gaming skills. I walk back to the explosion of Skittles I was sweeping up in Unit 1 and sigh.

'Internet Café' is just an umbrella term, really. We don't serve any food or beverages in the shop precisely because of incidents like this. A seemingly harmless spill here and there can ruin a perfectly good CPU faster than you can say 'Oops'.

I chuck the unfortunate Skittles into the trash and retreat behind the counter, where Dad is still on the phone with the customer representative from our Internet provider. There has been an intermittent interruption lately, and with how much we're paying for the service, it's unacceptable.

'Yes, yes, please send the technician right over. I'm hosting a big event next week and I can't have all these mishaps popping up.' Dad pauses. 'Okay, thank you. I'm counting on it.'

'They said the exact same thing yesterday.' He props a cheek on his fist after hanging up. 'Fingers crossed.'

'They'll follow through, Dad. Don't worry about it.'

'They'd better.' He rubs his temples. 'So, we good with all of these files so far?'

He nods at the Excel sheet on the monitor in front of us behind the counter. I still don't believe my father will be getting that weird chest pain he's been anticipating since my graduation ceremony any time soon, but there's no harm in indulging him. Besides, I do want to learn all about running the shop too—it's just mega hard to concentrate with this whole Lena thing nagging at me in the back of my mind.

'Yeah. My brain's not exploding just yet, so we're still good.'

'Don't be cute. We've only just begun.' Dad opens a new sheet, this time with a whole bunch of new data that look like some form of foreign language to me. 'You all set for your big event?'

'I guess,' I say. 'Mom's picking up your coat from the dry cleaners as we speak.'

Dad simply stares at me for a while.

'You don't have to stress about the scholarship so much, Nat. Your Mom and I, we can handle your tuition. We have enough saved up just in case.'

'I know.'

'And if your career doesn't work out, you will always have this, you know?' He gestures around us. 'We might not have much, but it's a fallback. And I'm not saying you can't do it, because I know you can, but just in case the worst happens . . .'

I fixate on the drawers in front of my father with all the paperwork stuffed inside, the bills and the fees and the instalments and all the things I'm too inexperienced to know about. 'I know,' I repeat. 'Thanks, Dad. Really. But I'll do my best to get that scholarship. It's a load off for you and Mom, and I *want* to work at Tala Tales Games.'

Dad smiles at me, and it's the first time I notice the wrinkles around his eyes, happy and tired at the same time. 'You're a good kid, Nat. You're going to make it big someday.'

'As my biological parent, you're obligated to say that.'

'And you're obligated to believe it,' he grins. 'Now, as your biological parent, I'm also obligated to know who may or may not be the mother of my future grandchildren . . .'

I go red. 'Dad, don't.'

'What?' He winks at me. 'That little moment I witnessed last night doesn't just happen to anyone.'

'It's not . . .' I bite my lip. 'It's not what you think it is.'

'What do you mean?' He frowns.

I stare at the squiggly lines floating about on the monitor of the unused unit in front of us.

'Nat.' Dad lowers his tone. 'I know you might feel like you and Lena are meant to be together—and if you two do end up giving me tons of grandkids, that's great. But are you sure you're going about this whole thing the right way?'

Great. First Josh, and now my own father.

'I'm not going to make your decisions for you, because I just want you to be happy. But if you're set on Lena, then you should at least tell her how you feel.'

I raise an eyebrow at him.

'If someone had all these feelings for you, you'd want to know, wouldn't you? You owe that to Lena. She deserves that much. Why are you so afraid?'

Because it's Lena. Because she's into this other guy who's way better than I am at everything and she'll probably reject me and I'll just die and burn to a crisp under the fiery Sun God's wrath and never be seen or heard of again.

Because she'll crush my heart.

Because I'll lose her.

Because I wouldn't know what to do if I did.

'When the time is right, you'll know.' Dad gives my shoulder a comforting squeeze. 'And if she doesn't feel the same way, then at least you won't be left wondering forever, right? Don't be afraid that things are going to change. Your friendship is strong enough to handle a little hurdle like this.'

Is it?

I think about Lena leaving and me alone, standing outside the sidewalk grillery amid empty seats and barbecue smoke.

'For what it's worth, Nat,' Dad says, 'it's always nice to know that someone loves you, don't you think?'

* * *

Here is a code that tells the computer how to make a decision. It may all seem overwhelming, but at its core, it is basically a logic puzzle—one that needs basic logic to solve.

In my room that night, I frown at the handout from the quick lecture today, as we've got another bonus assignment that checks if we're logical enough to, well, make a decision. I know I'm supposed to be submitting these 'bonus assignments' even if they're not a requirement, but I've been slacking off because concentrating just seems physically impossible.

It is always helpful to conceptualize what you need to code before you actually code. Let's start with a simple 'Yes' or 'No' problem. In this flowchart, we will tackle one simple question: Did you do the right thing today?

The notes then proceed to branch out with other questions like 'Did you accomplish your goal' or 'Did anyone get hurt in the process', landing in answers that either congratulate me for making the right choice or tell me to go back and rethink my decision.

I grit my teeth and fight the urge to rip the handout to shreds. It's definitely out to get me.

Setting the notes aside before I get a migraine, I turn back to my computer and start Googling more strategies for *Mitolohiya*. The networking night isn't the be-all-and-end-all of the programme, but given my track record for the programming assignments, I'll need all the top-notch gaming skills I can get to compensate.

The thing is, Lena telling me about diverging from the programming path should push me to focus on landing the scholarship even more, even without Lena. I know Dad was just being nice to me this morning, and I can't even imagine why he and Josh would both think Lena's not as perfect as she is. But his support aside, he did say he wants me to be happy, and making him happy will make me happy, so.

I *need* to make this scholarship work. It's the logical thing to do.

If only there were a code to program my brain into making the right decisions too.

Eight

In Which My Username
is Not Good Enough

A thin layer of clouds hijacks the entire sky the day before the mixer, and the overcast weather tints everything in an ominous glow. It's dull and grey everywhere I look, but I'd like to think it's just an unfortunate coincidence and not the universe telling me the odds aren't in my favour.

Besides, we've been idling in Mom's car while waiting for Lena for a while now, and there hasn't been a single drop of rain yet. I have a feeling the clouds will part and the sun will shine and the birds will sing and angel choirs will serenade us with divine hymns the moment Lena arrives.

In my head, at least.

'Now, remember. I'm entrusting a teenage girl's safety to you, honey. I trust you, and I know you won't make any bad decisions because you're my little boy and my little boy isn't foolish enough to disappoint me.' Mom raises a stern eyebrow and jolts me out of my thoughts. 'Are we clear on this?'

I open my mouth to reply when a head pops up behind us in the backseat.

'Don't worry, Mrs C. I'll keep Nat on the straight and narrow.' Josh lays a noble hand on his chest. 'He screws up, he answers to me.'

I make a face just as Mom turns around at Josh. 'Hey, you. Little stowaway. Remind me again why you're here with us? Because when I spoke to them on the phone earlier, Dins and Clara sounded all too happy to hand you over and get rid of you.'

'My parents value my freedom above all else.' Josh wiggles his eyebrows. 'I am a newly graduated teen in the prime of his life and must therefore be allowed to soar and roam free.'

'I'll be a good boy, Mom.' I shake my head. 'Lena's coming out any minute now. Will the two of you please, *please* promise me you'll behave?'

'*Me?*' Josh lets out a mock-gasp. 'Why, I'll be on my best behaviour. Your lovely lady will be treated like a princess back here with me.'

'It'll be fine, sweetie.' Mom winks. 'You'll be *fine.*'

These two are hopeless.

The sound of the front door creaking open makes all three of us look out of the window of Mom's car, over to where *Ate* Ami and Lena are emerging from their house. The sisters stroll down the sidewalk where we are idling.

'Morning, Mrs Carpio.' *Ate* Ami smiles at my mother through the rolled-down window.

'Hi, Tita.' Lena climbs into the backseat. 'Thanks for the ride.'

Mom waves her hand, then turns back to *Ate* Ami.

'Amihan,' Mom greets her back with a sympathetic tilt of her head. 'How's your father today?'

'The flavour of the day is the *Star Wars* franchise on loop, thanks to Nat,' *Ate* Ami grins. 'It'll keep him busy 'til the sun goes down. He devoured the mangoes, though.'

'I'll have my husband send over a fresh batch.'

'Thank you, Mrs Carpio.'

'We'll take good care of Little Lena.' She nudges me. 'Won't we, Nat?'

Ate Ami peers at me in the passenger seat and smiles. 'I don't doubt it.'

I burn up.

'Alright,' Mom says as *Ate* Ami waves at us and heads back inside the house. 'Let's get this show on the road.'

By 'show', she means Lena and me heading out to the venue of tomorrow night's mixer along with a stowaway, and by 'on the road', she means the three-hour drive to the budget hotel we booked. Mom is dropping us off, and we'll be staying there tonight for convenience—she's going to be busy all day tomorrow and won't be able to drive us to the mixer.

Thankfully, the venue is right down the next street to the hotel. The accommodation that she booked for us includes two rooms—one for me and Josh and one for Lena—and a small common area. Even though I've got a YouTube unboxer tagging along with me, it's still my first ever out-of-town trip with Lena, alone with no adult supervision around.

It should be romantic but given how Lena's dropping from the programme after this, I am not looking forward to it.

We barely hit the highway when my two best friends start making a ruckus in the back.

'Hey, Josh.'

'Lovely Lena. It's been a while.'

'Last time I saw you, you were in line for two hours trying to get free milk tea down the street.'

'Right. I forgot you witnessed that. I'll have you know that the two hours I waited out in the scorching heat of the sun was time well spent.'

'If you say so.' Lena giggles. 'So did you hit 50K yet?'

'55K now and rising.'

'Unbelievable. How do you manage all your fame and fortune, oh great bulk_smash?'

'I'm the most popular kid in our school. Did Nat not tell you that? Nat, tell her I'm the most popular kid in our school.'

I sigh. 'Josh is the most popular kid in our school.'

'I'm also the most well-informed. You wanna know anything about Nat, from embarrassing stories to downright criminal activities, you come to me. I've got records dating as early as our pre-school years.' Josh peers at my mother through the rear-view mirror. 'Sorry, Mrs C. Your son's a secret delinquent. Cat's out of the bag.'

'Hmm. An undercover criminal. Wish my school is as intriguing.' Lena sighs just as Mom shakes her head. 'As for the secrets, I'll get back to you on that.'

'Cool. You wanna play Twenty Questions?'

'Naw. Thumb War?'

'Yesss!'

And just like that, Josh and Lena start squabbling like five-year-olds in the backseat of my mother's car. The brutal battle goes on amid wails of lament and triumphant cheers; thumbs sacrificed and egos bruised in the process.

To be honest, I kinda want to join in on the Thumb War too.

Instead, I feign coolness and shake my head like I'm disappointed in my juvenile friends. And then, Mom's gentle hand snakes its way over mine and squeezes.

I turn to her beside me and she's smiling.

You'll be fine, she mouths to me, repeating herself.

I try to smile back.

I'll be fine.

* * *

'Raf says I should text him the minute we check in.' Lena lays her phone down on the table and focuses her attention back to her half-eaten chicken wing. 'He'll send a car to pick us up.'

My jaw clenches. 'Okay.'

'Not sure where he's taking us, but he says it serves the best steaks in town.' Lena pops a greasy strip of chicken skin into her mouth. 'Josh, you should come too.'

'No, thanks. Fancy places aren't my thing.' Josh finishes up the rest of his quarter-pounder, crumpling the paper wrapper in his hand. 'I'd rather just hang out in the room.'

'Alone, and without your laptop?' I dip my fries into my sundae. 'Why are you tagging along again?'

'I already told you. Teenage freedom.'

'Sure. Let's pretend *that's* real.' I turn back to Lena. 'Do we *have* to push through with this dinner? I mean, we need to turn in early. You know, for the mixer.'

'The tournament isn't until tomorrow *evening*—that's why it's called a networking *night*,' Lena crushes my protests. 'Besides, Raf's looking forward to treating us over there. It'll be fun, okay?'

I finish the rest of my meal in silence. We're at one of those gargantuan gas stations fully equipped with rows and rows of cafes, souvenir shops, and fast-food joints dedicated to luring unwitting travellers on the road. While Mom is outside gassing up the car, the three of us decided to pop inside one of the fast-food restaurants to grab a quick meal.

Of course, the minute Raf found out about us heading out to the venue a night early (oh, because he and Lena are apparently texting each other updates about their lives all the time), he just *had* to offer to treat us to the so-called best steaks in town because why the hell not.

The mental image of him charming Lena and—God forbid— kissing her at the end of the night makes me sick. The image of any other guy kissing Lena makes me sick.

'Alright, I'm done here.' Lena gets up from the table. 'I'm grabbing a latte at the convenience store next door. Coffee?'

'Cappuccino, please, m'lady.'

'Right away, good sir. Nat?'

'I'm good.'

Lena nods, and as soon as she leaves, I lean closer to Josh on the table.

'Lena's dropping out of the programme.'

'What?' Josh frowns at me. 'But what about the scholarship?'

'She's letting all of it go. The programme, the scholarship, everything. She says she wants to be an audio engineer.'

'Okay. That's pretty cool.'

'No, it's not.' I frown at Josh. 'You don't understand. She's only doing all this because stupid *Raf's* been showing her around backstage. It can't be what she *really* wants.'

'Yeah? Did she tell you that?'

'She didn't have to. She says she spoke to *Ate* Ami about this, but she's obviously just swayed,' I say. 'I mean, we've been slaving over this scholarship application because it's a great way for her to ease up on expenses and contribute financially to her family. Then she suddenly decides to quit to pursue a career in sound mixing? It's only been her dream for like the last ten seconds.'

'I don't know, man. You're starting to sound awfully like a douche right now.' Josh nods at the direction Lena disappeared to. 'If she says that's what she wants, and her own older sister supports her, maybe you should too.'

'Look. I *know* Lena. As her friend, I should steer her away from any bad decisions if I can spot them a mile away.'

'As her *friend*, you should support her dreams, no matter how different they are from yours.'

'It's not even about that. This is her future we're talking about.'

Josh raises an eyebrow. 'Is it?'

'What's that supposed to mean?'

'Nat. You sure your violent reaction to this whole thing is purely out of concern for Lena's future? You sure you're not freaking out because things aren't going according to plan?' he asks. 'You sure it doesn't have anything to do with WhyNotCocoNat's hidden desire for Relentless_Lena, and her newfound friendship with celebrity voice actor TheRealApolaki?'

The fact that Josh put me and Raf in the same sentence makes me realize just how silly my IGN sounds. I mean, how can someone with an In-Game Name like WhyNotCocoNat beat someone called TheRealApolaki, anyway? 'Of course, it's about Lena's future. My own feelings have nothing to do with this.'

Josh stares at me for a while, then sighs. 'Alright. I'm coming with you to tonight's dinner.'

'Oh.' I blink at him. 'Okay. Cool. What made you change your mind?'

'You.' Josh chugs down the rest of his soda. 'I need to be there for moral support, and to make sure you don't do anything stupid.'

'Why would I—'

'They were out of cappuccino, Sir Joshua of the Great Thumb War of the North Luzon Expressway. Just regular brewed coffee for you.' Lena suddenly reappears inside the fast-food joint and hands Josh his cup. 'You owe me a fifty.'

'Only the crispest bill in my pocket for Queen Lena, Bane of Thumbs. Oh, and I'm coming with tonight.' Josh whips out a fifty-peso bill that's immaculate, crease-wise. He was not kidding.

'Why, thank you. This'll be revenge for the next time the vending machine overlords decide to reject me.' Lena slips the money into her wallet. 'Also, yes, cool, you're coming, great. I'll text Raf. Glad you're on board.'

'Why not?' Josh shrugs. 'It's a welcome distraction.'

I narrow my eyes at him and wait for him to clarify, but Lena raises her coffee cup at us and clears her throat.

'Ayt. You guys ready to go?'

'Yep.' Josh stands and Lena starts marching back out to where Mom is parked. As we follow her out the door, Josh lowers his voice at me.

'Be cool, Nat,' he whispers. 'Whatever happens tonight, we still have to ride all the way back home with Lena the morning after your mixer tomorrow night. You wouldn't want to mess anything up.'

* * *

'Thirty minutes tops.' Lena tosses the card key onto the sofa in the small common area of our budget suite later that evening. 'You boys freshen up if you need to. Raf's car should be here by then.'

Josh scoffs. 'Please, Lena. You're talking to an unstoppable YouTube rising star here. I'll be so fresh Raf won't know what hit him.'

Lena chuckles and heads straight for one of the two adjacent rooms. Mom gave me The Look again before she dropped us off earlier, searing her instructions into my brain and programming me to treat Lena only with respect and adoration this whole trip. Frankly, I don't need my mother trying to *Inception* her thoughts into mine—I already adore Lena way more than I should.

I follow Josh as he chucks his overnight bag onto one of the twin beds in the room he and I will be sharing for two nights, and then he promptly crashes face-down on the mattress. Despite what he just told Lena, he doesn't move a muscle.

'Hey, Rising Star. Get your crap together. Thirty minutes tops.'

When he doesn't reply, I pluck a pillow from my bed and hurl it at him. He still doesn't budge.

'What's up with *him*?' Lena hovers behind me in our doorway. 'Cold feet? Nervous to meet someone who's got loads more subscribers than he does?'

'Dunno.' I shrug. 'He just crashed into bed like a bad glitch.'

'Hmm.' Lena surveys the room. She squints at Josh's unmoving form, his face planted firmly into his pillow, his hand grasping his phone for dear life. Lena takes one look at his death grip on his phone and gasps.

'"A welcome distraction", he says?' Lena snaps her fingers, her eyes wide. 'By Bathala and the gods. He broke up with someone, didn't he?'

This time, it is my turn to widen my eyes at her. 'Yeah. Not too long ago. How . . .?'

'Woman's intuition. Bad breakup? Like, she was the breaker, and he was the breakee?'

I give her a sombre nod.

'No–no–no–no.' Lena kneels on the floor near Josh's head. 'If that's the case, this whole dinner thing was a bad idea.'

I feel like an ass for getting my hopes up at Josh's expense. 'So, we're cancelling?'

'It's too late for that.' Lena's jaw is set. 'But I've still got half an hour before the car gets here. Get ready to see some magic.'

'What?'

Instead of replying to me, she lays a hand on Josh's head and strokes his hair. Then, in the softest voice she can muster, she breathes out. 'Josh? Is everything alright?'

Miraculously, Josh mumbles a reply. 'No. Everything's a mess.'

'Why?' Lena goes on in that super melodic, super therapeutic tone. 'What happened?'

'This. This happened.' Josh raises a lifeless arm and opens a Spotify link on an email. It's a song by an artist named Dizzy.

'My life sucks.' He hits Play, and a haunting voice comes on.

Joshua's a Gemini.

He broke my heart.

In the absence of any musical instruments with only the singer's voice trembling through the first line, the song breaks my heart too.

I gape at Josh's crumpled form. 'Holy shit, dude.'

'Bea sent me this last night.' Josh rolls over on his back, clutching the phone to his chest. 'After days of complete radio silence since she ended things with me, she sends me *this*. No subject, no message, no nothing. Just this stupid song and this stupid melody and this stupid pain in my chest.'

It all makes sense to me now, why he told Mom he wanted in on this trip at the very last minute. 'A welcome distraction', indeed.

'She played me, man. Acted like it was a clean breakup and fed me all this bullcrap about her wanting to be free, and now she tells me I broke her heart,' Josh goes on in that flat, helpless tone, like the smallest push can send him over the edge. 'The worst part is that I don't even know what I did.'

'Okay, that's it.' Lena flexes her fingers like she is prepping for a game. 'Nat, head down to the lobby café and buy some ice cream. The sweet, sinful, sugary kind. I've got work to do here.'

'Hold on.' I wrestle control over the situation and fail. 'My best friend is dying of heartbreak right now, and you're getting rid of me by sending me out to buy *ice cream*? Are you for real?'

'Yes, and yes.' Lena rolls up her sleeves. 'When he's ready to numb the pain with toys and games or something totally cathartic and totally irresponsible, he'll come to you. Right now, I'm the one he needs. Now get.'

Lena glares at me with so much authority that I'm compelled to speed out the door with one last look at Josh on the bed.

When I get back with a tub of double chocolate ice cream— something the staff had to run down to the nearest store to get for me because they didn't have it at the lobby café—the song 'Joshua' by Dizzy is on loop, blaring at top volume from the room.

I burst through the door. Josh is bawling his eyes out. His head is on Lena's lap, and she's stroking his hair like he's a cat.

But the weirdest thing is that Josh—ugly tears and gross snot and all—is smiling.

'About time.' Lena gestures to me to hand her the tub, and she offers it to Josh, who sits up from the bed and dives right into it.

'Raf's car will be here any minute.' She stands up and dusts her hands, grinning. 'But my work here is done.'

Amid mouthfuls of chocolate in his mouth, Josh blurts out. 'Thanks, Lena.'

Lena winks at me, then saunters out of our room into hers.

I stare at Josh with my mouth hanging open. 'What just happened?'

'Lena happened.' Josh swallows another spoonful of ice cream. 'I don't know what kind of voodoo that was, but you should be careful. She could be an ancient superior being no man can ever conquer.'

'I *am* careful. *Too* careful. Whenever Lena's involved, it's like I keep tiptoeing around these shards of glass. And they're not even normal glass shards that just cut you and you bleed. They're supercharged, like, fatal.'

'Dude, are you even listening to me?' Josh sighs. 'I'm telling you to be careful about how you act and what you say to her not for your benefit. For hers. You spend all this time not wanting to get hurt when you should be worried about hurting *her*.'

'You know I would never do that.'

Josh licks some more chocolatey goodness off his spoon, keeping it in his mouth like a twisted gangster's version of a dangling cigar. The whole thing makes what he says next drip with an ominous warning.

'Hey. The road to hell, man. You know what it's paved with.'

Nine

In Which Life is Really, Really Crappy in PvP Mode

I stare at the three forks on my table.

When Raf said he was taking us to the best steaks in town, he wasn't kidding. Hordes and hordes of hungry customers have been lining up outside since we got here, but because we're VIP and stuff, we breezed right past the common folk a while back, and they glared at us self-important teenagers like we're entitled jackasses, and, frankly, I agree with them.

Because there are chandeliers and fancy floors and servers in full formal wear. There are heavy tablecloths and napkins shaped like fowl and glistening silverware. There are differently sized plates and courses I can't pronounce and three freakin' forks—forks I didn't even know how to use properly.

And then there's me, in my old jeans and messy hair and casual shirt that says, 'My Brain is AFK'.

With the way I freeloaded my way on Lena's eighteenth birthday, this whole dinner thing just feels like a gigantic slap in the face from one Rafael Antonio.

'She did! I'm not even kidding.' Raf leans back in his chair beside Lena and laughs. 'Before detention was over, Mrs Lozada—bless her soul—told me to think about these vocal shenanigans, and where I thought these stupid impressions would take me in the real world. If she could see me now, huh?'

Lena giggled at Raf's fascinating fourth grade story, her face all flushed across from me. I also can't help but notice that she keeps touching his arm every now and then like it's as natural as breathing.

'Still, it wasn't a smooth ride,' Raf goes on. 'I've already lost count of all the failed auditions I had before I landed my first big gig. I still get them to this day.' He leans closer to the table then. 'But the trick is to train your mindset. For me, a failed audition doesn't mean you're a terrible actor. It just means that you're not right for the job *for that particular role*, and if you keep going, you'll land the role that's best for you.'

'Inspiring,' Josh pipes in beside me. Miraculously, he seems to have fully recovered from his momentary bout of devastation a while ago and is now back to his usual self—at least, for the duration of this dinner. 'When it comes to subscriber count though, you got any tips for that?'

Raf engages him with a winning smile. 'It's all about content, Josh. Sure, you can be charming as hell with all your gimmicks and quirks, but at the end of the day, you need to be able to provide real, actual value to your subscribers, something that's worth their time and attention. Those two things are the most valuable commodities online, and when your followers give them to you willingly, you need to make it worth their while.'

'Content. Value. Time and attention. Gotcha.' Josh scribbles madly into his phone.

'This isn't a free consultation, Josh.' Lena rolls her eyes. 'You've been throwing those interview questions all evening.'

'Oh, I don't mind at all.' Raf raises his palm and deflects even the tiniest tension with ease. 'We all have a responsibility to our viewers and helping each other out just means better channels they can choose from.'

Oh, please. I fight the urge to barf, because we just consumed what is probably the most expensive steak dinner in history, and it would be a shame if I just threw it all up.

'What about you, Nat?' Raf turns to me. 'We've talked about Lena's audio dreams and Josh's video content. What's *your* passion? What gets you out of bed in the morning?'

The chance to see Lena again. 'Erm. My PlayStation, I guess. And *Mitolohiya.*'

'Right, right. That was a good match, if I say so myself.' Raf grins with a perfect set of teeth, draining any poison from me with a single look. 'How's the shop, by the way? How are Mr and Mrs Carpio doing?'

'Okay.' I hate that despite the grin that I desperately want to slug off his perfect face, Raf does seem genuinely interested in our respective lives. 'Dad's hosting a competition next week.'

'Awesome! You guys need free promotion, you let me know.'

'Cool. Thanks, Raf.'

'No biggie. It's all about the fans, you know?' Raf smiles, and it's all I can do not to rage-quit right there.

Be cool, Nat. This is a nice place. It's not the time to go full berserk on these good people.

'Never forget your roots. That's the key to handling fame. I mean, I was a fan too, once. Most people get a taste of celebrity life and turn into complete douchebags, but even from the very beginning, I told myself I wouldn't be like them. My motto was to keep my head low, do the work, and do it well. And if people like it, then that's just a bonus. So far so good, huh?'

Is this guy for real? Seriously. Who talks like that?

'Anyway, I hate to cut this pleasant evening short, but I do have an early start tomorrow. Plenty of press stuff before the actual mixer.' He glances at his watch—one of those smartwatches that look like traditional watches but have digital displays that I will never be able to pull off—and motions for the bill. 'But before I forget . . .'

He probes into the pocket of his trousers—nice ones because he's not slumming it in jeans like I am—and takes out a small velvet box. When he hands it to Lena, my heart actually stops because he's going to propose and Lena is too young, but she probably won't care and he's probably set for life already and they'll have little celebrity kids and they'll travel the world on conventions and stuff and Lena will forget that a Nathaniel Carpio ever even existed.

But when Lena opens the box—way fancier and more masterfully crafted than the small pouch I gave Lena on her birthday—I see that there is a small enamel pin inside.

'Diwatas Are My Friends' is engraved on it in quirky script, and Lena is elated.

'This is so cool! Thanks, Raf!' She smiles at him, and he smiles at her, and for a moment it feels like I'm intruding into a personal moment and I shouldn't be here.

I shouldn't be here at all.

Then, Raf breaks eye contact and fishes out another box, handing it to me this time. 'I got you one too, Nat. Think of them as sort of good luck charms for tomorrow night.'

Mine says, 'Don't Judge an Aswang By Its Cover', because in *Mitolohiya*, it's the humans who are the villains of the story, and if you unlock the 'Tabi-Tabi Po' skill—something that supposedly wards off malevolent forces for humans—it actually makes you stronger.

'Thanks,' I mumble. The server assigned to our table arrives with the bill then, which Raf settles with a flourish as the staff clears our plates. It's the perfect end to the night, if only it didn't make me feel like I'm always second-best.

'Sorry I didn't get you anything,' Raf says to Josh. 'I wasn't sure you were into *Mitolohiya* too.'

'Don't worry about it. Just send me something to unbox and I'm set.'

'Hmm. You know what? We can do a collaboration of some sort. What do you say?'

'I say when do we start?'

As Josh and Raf launch into an excited conversation about live streams, Lena promptly pins her gift on her collar. Because I don't want to be rude or anything, I do the same thing.

But even as Raf and Josh are jabbering animatedly about a joint feature next month, out of the corner of my eye, I catch Lena gazing at Raf in pure admiration. I don't think she's ever looked at me that way.

In this real-life game of Player vs. Player, it's clear that I don't stand a chance.

Not even a little bit.

* * *

'I need to be alone for a while.' Josh crashes into bed the moment we get back. I guess whatever ancient spell Lena cast on him a while ago is only good for a couple of hours. 'My chest is collapsing into itself again.'

'Come on, Josh. Let me in.' I watch as he promptly puts *Joshua* on loop on his phone again. 'You gotta talk to me about this.'

'I will. Don't sweat it. I'm feeling better, but I just need to wallow for a bit. You know, lament my tortured fate.' Josh winces when the words 'wish I was too preoccupied to fall apart' comes on. 'Hang out in the living room for a bit, will you? That'll help me out. Promise.'

I let out a deep sigh. 'Whatever you say, man.' Right before I shut the door, I catch a certain something glistening in Josh's eyes.

I take a step toward the common area, but something about Raf handing Lena that little velvet box makes me feel like my insides are consuming themselves from within. I grit my teeth, step toward Lena's room instead, and knock.

'Lena? Okay if I come hang out for a bit?'

'Hey, Nat,' her muffled voice calls out from inside. 'Come on in.'

Lena's lying down on her tummy in bed, still in that nice little dress she was wearing at dinner, her legs swinging back and forth in the air. She's tapping away in a frenzy on her phone—I'm pretty sure it's a clicker game—but my eyes immediately zero in on her chest facing me, her neckline giving me a subtle little peek at her cleavage.

I look away.

'Josh isn't doing so well.' I find a spot by the edge of her bed with my back to her. 'He's playing that song again like he wants to torture himself to death with it.'

'Yeah?' Lena puts her game down and crawls to the edge of the bed with me. 'Maybe I should go over there.'

'He says he wants to be alone for a bit. Or, more accurately, I was kicked out.'

'Oh.' She settles in a seated position. 'It'll be okay, Nat. He'll make it through eventually. The human heart is stronger than you think.'

My gaze flutters to the night table beside her bed, where Lena has scattered a few personal effects on top of it. There is the velvet box from Raf, a copy of our card key, and the wallet I gave her two Christmases ago, now tattered and worn. She keeps a picture of her and *Ate* Ami in there, a photo I took of them during *Ate* Ami's promotion party.

It was especially cold that night, and I remember Lena snuggling close to me at dinner whenever she could for body warmth. The closer she got though, the more my chest constricted, like my own body knew we were not meant to be.

So yes, the human heart can be strong and resilient, but when it comes to small, seemingly insignificant moments like those, it just as easily breaks.

'You think you'll be ready for the tournament tomorrow night?' Lena disrupts my thoughts. 'I heard the matches are random. You can even get matched up with someone from the same school.'

'Guess we'll see tomorrow.' I shrug. 'I'm not worried, though. I have a good teacher.'

'A teacher who would like to be compensated with free chicken inasal for a week.'

'That can be arranged.'

Lena smiles at me with a brightness that reaches her eyes, and with the way her head is tilted to one side and her hair is falling down her shoulders, there is just no possible way for me not to catch my breath. I don't even remember a time before I was completely smitten. Was there even a time? It just seems like the farthest memory I can remember was standing at the edge of the end, at that point where everything became a before and an after.

That very first morning of the six-peso coin, it was just like any other day. I had classes to go to and homework to finish and a particularly annoying group project my science classmates weren't helping me with. But then the bell rang, and I waited for her at the sidewalk grillery. As I was picking out our favourites from the five-item menu, she popped up beside me in her school uniform and her ponytail and her bright, bright smile, and all I remember was that her smile was so beautiful it made my heart hurt.

I dated a girl from my school Before Lena (B.L.). She helped me with a math problem I was having a hard time solving, and even after I aced the exam, we just kept hanging out and became a thing after that. It was probably just because she was the first girl who ever showed any interest in me, but with her it was just heaps and heaps of hormones and wanting to see how it felt like to kiss a girl.

So, she kissed me in the local cinema one day, and I kissed her back. It was nice. Then that was it.

Josh told me then that if all I ever felt was lust, then maybe I'm not being fair to this girl, and I wasn't. We never got any farther than that.

But with Lena, it's . . . different. I always thought I knew how my own body operated B.L., but when she came along, it's like everything I've ever known about myself turned out to be a lie. Because with Lena, I just . . . want to be near her. To connect her soul with mine. And that would be enough.

But there is a science to heartbreak, they say. And if we're apart from someone, we just ache and ache and ache like we're desperate for nourishment but can't have it. I guess that's how it feels, every single day, being with Lena but not being with her, so close together yet still miles and miles apart.

It takes a while for me to realize that as I'm gazing at Lena's face in silence like this, she's grown quiet too.

Time for a quick awkward thing to say.

'So, those steaks were good.'

'Uh-huh.' She smoothens out her skirt over her thighs. 'I couldn't get enough.'

'Yeah. I could've sworn I saw a little trace of Dizon the Devourer in there, just itching to burst out.'

'Naw. It wasn't the time and place. She happens to like value-for-money inasal. Those trump fancy steaks any day.'

Hoping she meant me over Raf, I feel bolder somehow. 'It's not about the bill.'

'Definitely not.'

'If Raf wanted to treat you someplace nice, he should have asked me.'

'You do know my tastes best.'

'Grilled chicken all day, every day.'

'Mmm. Heaven.'

'We could stay in like, a little pocket of the universe, just me and you.'

'That sounds nice.'

With my heart drumming in my ears, I lean closer. 'We'll live off of 'em until the world ends and stuff.'

Surprisingly, she doesn't move away. 'Zombie apocalypse.'

'Or monsters could arrive.'

'Like *Mitolohiya*.'

'And we wouldn't give a damn.'

'We wouldn't.'

Breathing down on Lena's face like this, I realize I've lowered my voice to a whisper, and she hasn't moved an inch. If I shifted my body to face her properly, her skin would be right against mine, flesh on flesh and heat on heat. If we moved even closer, I don't think I can hold myself back a second longer from what I might do next.

My chest throbs.

My stomach churns.

My eyes flicker down to her lips.

Then, the bomb.

'My mother came to visit me yesterday.'

Everything shifts. 'Crap.'

'Yeah. Crap.'

I inch away from her. 'What did she want?'

'Redemption,' she whispers. 'Or money. I don't know. After years and years of ghosting us, she hears about my graduation, and suddenly decides she wants to take me away. To take care of me. To be a mom.'

'Oh, man.'

'She said she's got this condo downtown, and it's right beside this good university and near her workplace, and she can pick me up and drop me off every day and be the mother-and-daughter team she thinks I want us to be. She said they're not legally separated, Dad and her, and that she can easily make arrangements and have me live with her without having to involve any of the courts in our affairs.'

'What did you tell her?'

'I told her it's too late.' Lena's face is ashen. 'I told her I didn't want her in my life, not when she was never in ours. Not when she left *Ate* Ami to fend for herself and Dad to waste away in our living room and me clueless about her, too young to understand anything but old enough to understand she didn't love us. I told her to piss off, essentially.'

Lena tries to smile, but things are pooling up inside her and threatening to burst. 'She can't just swoop in and try to save the day when we're already doing fine on our own. She doesn't get to do that. I'm mad at her, obviously. But what I don't understand is how I can be mad at someone I don't even know.' She bites down on her lips. 'So maybe I'm angry at her, or not. Or maybe I'm just angry at the way she makes me feel.'

I wrap an arm around her shoulders and squeeze, tossing my own feelings aside. 'I'm sorry, Lena.'

'Nat.' She lets out a weak laugh. 'I rant to you about my mother, and you apologize? You've always been too nice for your own good.'

'Sorry. I mean, uh, okay.'

She giggles, then lays her head against my shoulder. There is a skewed sense of time in my head now. I fight the urge to plant a kiss on her head.

We stay that way for a while. We breathe together and feel together in silence, the faint, muffled sound of Josh's looped music weaving in from the other room. My emotions rip a hole through me, stripping me of my defences.

'Hey, Nat?'

'Yeah?'

She shifts her position to look up at me and doesn't say anything. She keeps staring at me and I keep staring at her and I'm trembling, every fibre of my being coming undone, going off in all the wrong places.

Then, she kisses me.

Lena kisses me.

I always thought that kissing Lena would make my body come alive, like just the feel of her skin and the touch of her lips would send me into an overdrive I can't recover from. I always fantasized how soft and wonderful it would all be, a dream and a celebration of reality all at the same time.

But when Lena lands her lips on mine, it feels . . . wrong.

She pushes her body against me, and I plunge back down on her bed with a grunt, her soft curls cascading down my face. She pins me down and kisses me hard and my mind is a blank. A soft gasp escapes her lips against mine, but everything still feels wrong, wrong, wrong.

Then, something warm and wet trickles down to my cheek, and Lena is crying. She's *crying*.

It takes everything I have to gently push her away.

'Lena, I'm so sor—'

'Don't.' She recoils. 'Nat, please. Don't apologize.'

'I—'

'I did this. Don't apologize or you're just going to make me feel worse.'

'Lena, please.' I try to take her hand, but she pulls away. It scratches my skin raw. 'Please tell me what's wrong.'

'Nothing. I just . . . wanted to see something.' She rubs her eyes hastily with the back of her fist. 'I think you should leave now.'

'Lena—'

'Please leave, Nat.' I can barely hear her voice. 'Please.'

And I sit there beside her and wonder how I screwed this up so badly when all I ever wanted was to be there for her and keep all the loneliness at bay. But I get up, walk to the door, and leave. Just like she wanted me to.

Josh has cried himself to sleep. There are caked tears around his swollen eyes and he's hugging a pillow firmly against his chest, his eyes shut tight and his brows furrowed. I drape the covers over him and shut off the music on his phone, but not before one line from the song latches onto my head long after I turned the music off.

Funny how my world could end,
In silence.

Ten

In Which I Wish Bad Decisions Had a Money-Back Guarantee

'Batman and Wonder Woman.' Josh stuffs half a slice of pizza in his mouth the next morning. 'This comic book forum I'm in, they let me read this thing where Wondy tells Bats they can't be together because she's eventually gonna outlive him, so she breaks up with him for his own good.'

I raise an eyebrow at him.

'What?' he shrugs. 'I told you I know stuff. And yes, I have other friends.'

'So, you're saying that Lena doesn't want to be with me for my own good?' I reposition a fallen pepperoni onto my own slice of pizza. 'Is she supposed to be Wonder Woman in this situation?'

'Obviously.'

'I'm not Batman, Josh.'

'Darn right you're not. You're nowhere even near his coolness level.'

'You forget that I'm cool enough to spend all my time on this trip with a heartbroken dude who plays with toys all day and posts videos of his hands opening boxes online.'

'Okay, well, there's that.' Josh pops a pepperoni into his mouth. The pizza's dry, but we didn't feel like leaving the room and Lena had already left mysteriously before we even got up, so we decided to have some pizza delivered for lunch.

It tastes terrible.

'Didn't she say she wanted to "see something"? Maybe she wanted to check if she could . . . feel things. Like, feel something for you. You know, because of the whole "I can't be with you but I'm still kinda curious" thing,' Josh says. 'Hence the weird kiss and the vicious attack on you.'

'She didn't *viciously attack me*,' I sigh. 'She was upset. She probably just . . . needed some comfort.'

'In your mouth?'

'Your mozzarella's sliding off.'

'Dammit.'

Josh busies himself with all the precious mozzarella escaping his meal, and my fingers subconsciously touch my own lips.

Lena kissed me. She kissed me last night, and I held her close, and we were on her bed and things got . . . weird. I should be ecstatic, but I'm not.

'Listen, Nat,' Josh says, when the mozzarella incident seems to be under control. 'I know Lena is a good friend—she's awesome at consoling breakup victims, and her Thumb War game is on point. But I still stand by my opinion—I don't think you're the right guy for her.'

'Josh.'

'Just indulge me for a sec.' He straightens up. 'Let's do an exercise here. I want you to list down Lena's flaws for me.'

'Come on.'

'I mean it. I want you to give this some serious thought. Look past all the perfection you see.'

I look down. Lena's flawed for sure—she's an actual human being, for goodness' sake. She doesn't have a very pleasing personality when it comes to her peers, which is why she doesn't have any close friends in her own school. She's a little too intense sometimes, and she's often so absorbed in the music from her headphones that she barely gives a crap about the world around her.

She has no problems fitting in, though—she's not an outlier, so there are no odd quirks there. She gets good-enough grades, likes dresses as much as Chucks, and is up to date with K-pop stuff as much as the next person. She doesn't share those things with me since she knows I know nothing about it, but she has *Ate* Ami to gush with her in that respect.

So, really, Lena is just Lena—nothing more, nothing less.

'It's pointless. Why do I feel like the cracks make the vase more beautiful?'

'Think about it, Nat. You told me she wanted to carve her own path out of her own merit, but she has been letting Raf take her to backstage passes and other special perks, right? That's a little hypocritical of her. I think it's great she wants to be an audio engineer and live a life that's not tied down to you. But she shouldn't have led you on with that kiss.'

'Come on, Josh. You can't do that. You can't make her out to be the villain here. You're making it sound like she's diabolical for wanting to chase her dreams.'

'She's *not* the villain, you idiot. Sure, she's making mistakes and bad decisions along the way, but she's doing what she wants and needs to do as the hero of her own story. Why can't you do the same with yours?'

I scarf down the last of my pizza and sigh. 'Did you get a fresh batch of buffs today? You're pretty enlightened for someone who just got dumped.'

'Guess that's what being a dumpee does to me. Some get haircuts and move to a different country. I, apparently, dish out words of wisdom to hopeless gamers who are in love with their best friend.'

I stare hard at the lonely crumbs at the bottom of the empty pizza box, and they stare right back.

'What Bea did. Messing with you like this?' I look back up at Josh. 'It's her loss. You know that, right?'

Josh steels himself, like he's suddenly guarding his personal space and the half-eaten slice in his hand. 'Is it? 'Coz it sure doesn't feel that way.'

'Hey, I'm no expert. All I know about this thing is Nathan Drake and Elena Fisher's epic love.' I shrug. 'All I'm saying is if she broke up with you because she got fed up with all the toys, then maybe she wasn't The One too, you know? I mean, when you're already committed to each other in a relationship, you're supposed to grow together, not outgrow each other, right?'

Josh blinks across the room at the phone on his bed. 'Maybe.'

'Maybe.'

He lets out a long, drawn-out breath. 'You should really rethink your whole perspective on love, man. This isn't *Uncharted*.'

'Yeah.' The memory of Lena in tears last night squeezes my insides. 'It's not.'

Josh takes a good whiff of the pizza in his hand before taking a huge bite.

'Seriously, though.' I lay a hand on his shoulder. 'Are you going to be okay alone here tonight? The mixer might take a while.'

'I'll be fine. This is my vacation too, remember? I'll probably order the all-meat variant next.'

'Which reminds me.' I get up and rummage around in my backpack for the two Ziploc bags Mom shoved into my belongings yesterday. 'I have more Superman sandwiches for you.'

Something wet and trembling pools against Josh's eyes for a bit, then he blinks it away. 'I'd really like that.'

* * *

Blown up against the wall of the event hall right under the big banner that says 'Tala Tales Games Networking Night' is our group photo taken during that official press photo day, and I look like a man possessed.

One eye is halfway closed while the other is looking up at something at the ceiling that was apparently more interesting than the camera at the time, and the photographer chose this exact moment to take the photo. Of all the smiling, prim-and-proper candidates in the shot, I am the only one who looks like a complete doofus.

'I wouldn't worry about it,' says Kyle, one of the other finalists from my school. 'They're not going to pick students based on the group shot alone, right?'

Easy for him to say. He's right there front and centre in the shot, beaming like an ad for whitening toothpaste. 'Yeah,' I grumble. 'I guess not.'

'Boys, please.' Mrs Diwa waves an exasperated hand at us, gesturing us to Table 10. 'Take your seats. Where are the twins?'

'Marko is over there by the buffet table.' Kyle squints across the hall. 'And is that . . . Maria talking to the CEO?'

'Oh, for the love of—' Mrs Diwa lets out a long sigh and squeezes between the crowd toward where Maria is waving her arms animatedly at some guy in a fancy suit. She has always been the most ambitious of us all, so it only makes sense that the first thing she would do is chat up the CEO.

'I don't know why Mrs Diwa is all worked up about it,' Kyle says as we both settle into our seats. 'I mean, it's a networking night, right? We should be out there networking.'

'She probably just doesn't want to take any chances.' I adjust the uncomfortable tie on my father's oversized coat. 'Mrs Diwa has a lot riding on this. We've got the most number of reps from the same school.'

'Do we?' Kyle plucks the card propped up in the middle of our small round table. 'Huh. Check this out. It's our tournament matchups.'

I peer at the card. Instead of a menu or a programme, the card lists the names of the remaining finalists and all the pairings for the night. Because the event is not going to last forever, the whole thing isn't built to be a tournament, with brackets and elimination rounds. Instead, we're all randomly matched with some other finalist, and winners of each match are scored for overall ability, like tactics used and creativity and Actions Per Minute and such. The points are all tallied at the end of the night, and whoever gets the highest score wins.

My eyes scan the colourful card and see that I'm up against some guy named Oliver from a regional high school.

'Well, I have no idea who any of these are,' Kyle says. 'Guess that makes it easier to own them, right?'

I don't know Kyle very well except that we're in the same batch, but I do know his APM is legendary. 'Yeah. It's just a friendly match, anyway. No pressure.'

'Tell that to Maria.'

We spot poor Mrs Diwa standing beside Maria with her hands clasped to her sides, her nerves wrecked and fraying all over the place. Maria, on the other hand, is still laughing with the CEO of Tala Tales Games, all casual and chill, while Mrs Diwa looks like she's ready to dive in between them in case Maria says something inappropriate.

Meanwhile, the wayward twin Marko is still stuffing his face at the *lechon* station.

'I'm going to take a leak,' I say. 'This whole thing is making me nervous.'

'When you gotta go, you gotta go.' Kyle shrugs and whips out his phone.

I lace through the tables to look for Lena and spot her sitting at Table 4, near a glass door that leads to an outdoor garden. She's staring at the flowers through the glass while chewing on a chunky piece of chicken from her plate, a sticker name tag labelled 'Elena Dizon' taped to her forehead.

She's alone at last. I haven't spoken to her since the awkward thing last night, and when I walked here from our hotel, she and Raf were chatting like reunited long-lost cousins. Somewhere along the way, Raf bumped into me, charmed the pants out of all my schoolmates and teachers, and genuinely wished me luck before heading off on more PR stuff. I hate how nice he is to everyone.

But now here's Lena, alone and still as heartbreakingly beautiful as she was in her room last night.

'Hey.' I whisper near her ear, and she gives a little start. 'Okay if I sit here?'

'Oh god, please.' Lena rolls her eyes as I pull up the chair beside her. 'If it weren't for these chicken nuggets, I would have died of boredom.'

I scan the three other students at the table, each of them preoccupied with their phones or their plates. From her name tag, I notice that the girl seated on Lena's other side is from her school too, but they are acting like complete strangers.

'You look . . . awesome,' I stammer, keeping my eyes trained on the piece of chicken on her plate.

'Right back at you, slugger.' Lena reaches over to straighten my tie. 'You clean up nice.'

'Dad's old clothes to the rescue,' I say. Judging from the way she's behaving, we're apparently going to act like last night didn't happen. I'm down with that. 'Have you seen the match card?'

'Yep. I know the guy you're up against—I saw his online playthrough once. He's no match for you, Nat.' Lena tilts her head and smiles at me. 'You're going to win. I just know it. You deserve this more than anyone.'

A few laptops are set up across a long table up front, itching for the *Mitolohiya* matches to begin. Against the front wall is a huge LED screen that is currently looping a video presentation of Tala Tales Games' history, how it all began with four guys in their college dorm room and how it grew to the trendsetting brand it is today. As one of the biggest pioneers of the Philippine video game industry, the company has been steadily producing quality content both here and abroad, including top-rated mobile apps and other genres like the recent *Mitolohiya* spin-off, *Engkanto Land: Diwata Party MOBA*.

It's a revolutionary company, and I want to be a part of it. But Lena's not going to be there with me.

All the feelings churning inside me start bubbling up to the surface, and there's nothing I want more than to tell Lena everything, everything, everything.

But someone clears her throat behind me, and I look up.

'Back to your seat, *hijo*.' A grumpy woman shoots me a stern look. She rips Lena's nametag from her forehead in one swift motion and tapes it properly to Lena's chest, making her wince. 'The programme's about to start.'

'Umm. Okay.' I get up and Lena throws me a thumbs-up sign. I flash her a weak smile and head back to my seat, defeated.

Table 10 is fully occupied with three other people now, plus Maria sulking in her seat beside Mrs Diwa and Marko still not done with his *lechon*.

'Pretty long bathroom break,' Kyle says as I slump back down beside him. 'You feeling okay?'

The lights dim, but I can still see Lena across the hall at the corner table, the longing inside me as piercing as ever.

'No, Kyle.' I sigh. 'I feel like absolute crap.'

* * *

Crap. Crap, crap, crap.

I select my Manananggal troops and scatter them in different directions as fast as I can, bracing myself as Oliver casts his Kidlat Shower spell over the general area. The Engkanto Clan is known for its deadly Area of Effect spells that my Aswang units are weak against, and getting caught within range can instantly drain my units' health bars and cripple my offence.

I click back to my base and start producing more Manananggal to make up for the ones I've lost—they've been valiant, and I'm grateful for their service. But the in-game notification tells me I've lost another horde, and it's no use. Building more units will take up too many resources—resources I no longer have.

This is where I always wish I could hear the shoutcaster's commentary just to get an inkling of what Oliver is up to behind my back.

But I can't. With my headphones on, I can't hear anything, I'm all alone, and there's nothing but the sound of my own heartbeat drumming in my ears. I've got no eyes on Oliver's base, and I can't afford to lose any more troops.

So, I go back to the basics. With my remaining resources, I mass produce my Sigbin for all they're worth—small, cheap, squishy, but efficient. It's not the smartest strategy to use the most basic units toward end game, but this is all I have left, and I've never been one to switch things up too radically when push comes to shove.

With everything that's left, I separate my Sigbin into multiple control groups and send them out in all directions, multitasking like crazy. It's all or nothing—I will either surprise Oliver with such an unexpected move, or this huge risk will have zero payoff at all. In fact, it might even be my ultimate downfall, which means I've got the most powerful weapon no amount of fear or anxiety can beat.

I've got nothing left to lose.

I send my Sigbin to dash around the spirit mages and eliminate the spellcasters as quickly as I can, then send what's left of my Manananggal right back on track for the attack on his base, because getting back up on my feet is crucial, especially during end game. My attack comes from way out of left field, and my groups of Sigbin surprise Oliver so much he sends his spellcasters out of his base for another barrage of Kidlat Showers.

Which is where he makes his ultimate mistake.

My Sigbin surround his mages and they chomp down on their HP with ease, ridding him of his whole spellcaster army in mere seconds. The excitement of the crowd behind me reaches a fever pitch as I break into Oliver's stronghold, crushing his defences with my Tikbalang and Kapre combo units. In a last-ditch attempt to repel my advances, Oliver summons Juan Tamad—special character and Engkanto Clan ally—to help with his defence.

But I didn't come this far to lose, not when there's so much on the line.

So, I sacrifice my remaining Sigbin to lure his hero away. Then, my Kapre unleashes a barrage of relentless blows on his command post until it whittles down to its last health bar.

It crumbles to the ground.

The word 'VICTORY' flashes on my screen and there is a roar of applause behind me, and the host up front says something I can't quite catch. Because my heart is still pounding in my ears, because my fingers are still shaking, because there's nothing more nerve-wracking than the pressure of wanting something so, so badly.

I stumble away from the laptop as the next match is announced, and my schoolmates pat me on the back as soon as I reach them in the crowd.

'Taking a leak?' Kyle grins at me.

I nod, and he guffaws. 'You deserve it, man. Go wild.'

I disappear into the crowd that is pushing and pulling in the excitement of the next round, desperate for Lena's smiling face in a sea of strangers. Then, like a beacon of light clearing through the fog in my muddled mind, I see her.

She's standing by the glass door exit near her table, pointing to her ear, telling me it's too loud in here to carry out a proper conversation. She pushes open the glass door to the garden and motions for me to follow her.

The moment we step out into the crisp night breeze and the glass door swings shut, the din from the event hall comes to an abrupt stop. Out here, it's just the evening crickets in the haze of summer and the smell of freshly cut grass in the yard.

It's perfect.

'What did I tell you?' Lena smiles. 'Those moves were unlike anything I have ever seen.'

'The long hours of losing to you over and over again have paid off.' I grin. 'I can't believe you still won your match though, even though you obviously threw the game.'

'No minor feat.' She giggles. We settle down on a stone bench surrounded by a low santan hedge, and Lena stretches out her legs in front of her. After a satisfying yawn, she leans her hands back behind her, gazing up at the sky.

'I met some of the people back there when Raf took me to the recording studio. They're outsourced by Tala Tales Games, so they don't have much of a pull here, but they said they can try and see if they can get some of their colleagues at this other company to meet with me. You know, just to have a teeny tiny foot in the door.'

Upon hearing Raf's name again in a moment as intimate as this, my emotions start pushing, violent and desperate.

'Pretty cool, isn't it? And I have Raf to thank for it. It's too bad he's working right now and had to leave early. He would have loved to hang out.'

Maybe it's the jealousy or the garden or the adrenaline still pumping through my veins, but I finally speak up.

'Don't do it.'

Lena blinks her confusion at me. 'What?'

'The scholarship. Don't give it up. You've worked so hard, you're this close, and you can't just give it up for a sudden interest in sound mixing.'

'Sudden interest?' Lena steels herself. 'If you think this is a *sudden interest*, then you don't know me at all.'

'That's not what I mean. It's just—what's sudden is—' I shift my body to face her. 'It's Raf. He's showing you all these things and introducing you to all these people . . . I just think maybe it's a distraction. You know, from . . . from what you really want.'

Lena doesn't tear her eyes away. 'And what do I really want, Nat?'

This isn't going well. 'The programme. The scholarship. The security and stability. Doing what we love. It's what we both want . . .' My voice falters. '. . . isn't it?'

'It's what *you* want, Nat. It's what *you* love. *Mitolohiya* is fun, yes, but at the end of the day, it's not exactly what I want to *do* with the rest of my life, you know? I told you about this that night at the shop.'

'Yes, but that's exactly it. This all just came up a few nights ago, and it's all because you met Raf. If he hadn't introduced himself to you at the photo shoot, you never would've even considered leaving the programme.'

'How would you know, Nat? How would you know what I would or wouldn't have considered?' Lena grits her teeth. 'Don't you understand how grateful I am that Raf walked into our lives that day? How could you even say that!'

'Because! It's Raf!' I throw my hands up. 'Don't you see why he's doing all this?'

'No, Nat. Enlighten me. Why *exactly* is Raf doing all this?'

'Because he likes you, Lena! Why else would he keep swooping in like some big hero to try and impress you with all this fancy shit?'

Lena narrows her eyes. 'Sure, he likes me. Because God forbid he's doing all this because he's a nice person, because he actually wants to help, because he actually sees some *potential* in me, because I actually have some skill.'

'That's not—'

'God forbid that I'm actually good at it, because all I'm good for is sitting still and looking pretty. Is that it, Nat? Is that what you want to say? That the only logical, possible, definitive reason I'd be worth anything is because *Raf* likes me—'

'Damn it, Lena! You're you! How can anyone not like you?'

She falls silent, and I say the words I wish I never did.

'*I* like you, Lena. And I can't . . . I can't lose you.'

If we were anything like Nathan Drake and Elena Fisher, we would fight then make up and fall into each other's arms and ride off into the sunset toward another great adventure together— always together—forever.

But we are *not* Nate and Elena.

Instead, Lena slinks away from me, and it snags at an open wound in my side.

'Don't do that.'

'Do what?'

'This. This whole I-like-you thing, unloading all your feelings and making me feel guilty for dropping. You can't use your feelings for me to make me stay. You just can't. It's not fair.'

'Lena, I'm sor—'

'How dare you. How dare you tell me what I really want, what I can and can't do. How dare you use your feelings to manipulate me like this, when it took me this long to talk to you about my dreams exactly because I was scared of how you'd react. How dare you tell me that my dreams mean nothing, that all that matters is how *you* feel, what *you* want, and how *you* envision the future together.'

I feel lightheaded.

'You *can't* lose me? Well, tough—I was never yours to begin with.' She stands and blinks back the angry tears in her eyes. 'I don't owe you anything, Nat. I can't do this anymore.'

She speeds back to the glass door, and my body springs up to follow. 'Lena. Lena, *please*—'

She yanks the door open, and we're back inside and the roar of the crowd and the lights are on me and everyone's looking and I freeze in my place, because the host has just called my name, because they've just tallied the scores, because I've just won.

I won the tournament.

And people are clapping and cheering and my teacher is leading me to the stage and Lena is leaving. She's leaving, as I see her small form retreat into the back exits, away from all this, away from me.

The crowd closes in on us and between us, until she's gone and I'm still here.

More than anything else in the world, I want to go for the win and triumph over all this pain, but I can't.

Because I've already lost.

And all I had to do is be myself.

* * *

'Lena!'

It's too late.

I burst through the hotel room. 'Lena!'

You've lost her.

'Lena!'

She's already gone.

'Nat . . .' Josh appears in his doorway with a horrified look on his face, the ghost of my mistake.

I whirl around. 'Where's Lena?'

'Nat—'

'I messed up, Josh. I need to see her—'

'NAT!'

Josh steadies my shoulder with a firm grip.

'Mrs C called,' he says. 'Your dad's in the hospital.'

Stage Three: Win Elena Dizon's Heart

Eleven

In Which a Gameplay Walkthrough on Love Would Really Come in Handy Right Now

Game Concept Proposal by Nathaniel Carpio
Genre: Roguelite Dungeon-Crawler
A regular, unremarkable protagonist starts his journey on the first floor of the infinite dungeon, with no boons, buffs, or extra lives. He goes through the motions, dies over and over and over again, then starts over from scratch.

Eventually, after the nth time of trying, he reaches the 100th floor. He has a handful of buffs now, extra advantages and power-ups earned from the blood, sweat, and tears of each new run. He has bested every skeleton around the corner and every nasty goblin lurking in the shadows. He has dodged spiky traps and deathly pits; he has leaped over great ravines and the bottomless abyss. He is battle-damaged, bruised, and heartbroken. He is damaged beyond repair, and he's only got one life left.

But, because the game features procedurally generated levels and one wrong move can spell the difference between victory and defeat—or because the randomness of the dungeon just means that he's got the worst luck in the world—he makes one small miscalculation in his damage output and his HP, and, right before the final boss Raf Phase II, he dies.

125

He dies, and Lena is lost, and Raf wins, and Nat loses, and he has to start from the very beginning all over again, because life sucks and then you die.

'Thank you, ma'am. See you tomorrow.' I greet the customer with a smile as she leaves the shop and head right to her unit to clean up. I shut down open applications, set bulk_smash's wallpaper and screensaver, tidy up the station, push back a few chairs down the aisle. I make my way back behind the counter, where Dad throws me a look of concern.

'Erm. You okay there, Nat?'

'Peachy.' I nod toward Dad's checklist behind the register. 'Everything all set for the competition? The Internet guys haven't returned my call yet, have they?'

'Uh, no.' Dad blinks. 'Listen, son. Why don't you go get some rest? I'll take care of the technicians and—'

'S'okay, I got it. How are you feeling, Dad? How's the knee?'

'Peachy,' Dad mimics me with a smile.

'Any pain?'

'Nope.'

'Did you take your meds today?'

'Yes, yes.' Dad taps his knee. 'Don't worry, Nat. It's nothing your old man can't take.'

My eyes inevitably travel down to the wayward knee, and a tingling sensation sweeps up the back of my neck. I have been brushing off that 'weird chest pain' as my father's paranoid way of making sure I learn the ins and outs of the business, but as it turns out, it's not his chest we should be worrying about. All this time, there's this other silent culprit creeping through his body like the deceptive thief that it is.

Gout. Who would have thought?

That night during the tournament, I was so caught up in my selfish crap about Lena that I couldn't even pick up my own phone. It had to take Josh to knock some sense into me before everything morphed back into focus—Dad was rushed to the hospital because his knee hurt so bad that he couldn't walk. They injected him with something and gave him meds, and he should be okay now under monitoring, but I can't help but think that if it was something else, if it really was a weird chest pain and it wasn't just gout, then my father would've been—he would've—

I flinch. My chest feels tight.

'Nat?'

I shake my head, squeeze Dad's shoulder, and promptly swivel around before the heat behind my eyes turns into something else. I pick up the receiver and punch in the hotline number for our Internet provider.

Dad throws me another confused look before he shrugs and hobbles over to one of the unoccupied units.

Carpio Diem Internet Café's little *Mitolohiya* competition is coming up in a few days, and I've been throwing myself into prepping the thing non-stop. I feel very productive lately; plus, it's the best use of my time instead of sulking around because of the whole ruining-my-life-by-hurting-my-best-friend-and-pretty-much-making-sure-she-never-wants-to-talk-to-me-ever-again thing.

I mean, I'm not even sulking. It's been a week since the horrible mixer, where I won and got back to the hotel and Lena was gone because *Ate* Ami picked her up and took her home in the middle of the night. Lena has cut me off like a diseased zombie-infected arm ever since, avoiding my calls and staying the hell away from me as she should, because who am I kidding?

It's just me. Just good ol' Nat, baring his soul and offering his heart out to her like an open wound, declaring his stupid feelings and saying all these stupid things, hurting her and driving her away. It's just me. Nothing awesome. Nothing special.

To be honest, I wouldn't want to return my calls, either.

Besides, I've been slacking off, and I'm ashamed to say that it had to take Dad's hospital scare before I got my shit together. It's not all about Lena. It's not all about me.

So yeah. Like I said, I'm very productive. Mom and Dad need my help, and I'm stepping up to Dad 'showing the ropes' to me.

I think I'm doing a pretty good job, if I say so myself.

At least, until Mom steps into the picture.

She clears her throat as I'm dozing off in my room one day, PlayStation controller on my chest and streams of drool slobbering down my cheek. I jolt upright.

Mom is standing in front of my computer, staring at the blinking cursor on my completely empty, completely blank essay.

She sighs. 'This is my fault too. How we adapt to this world is defined by our upbringing, and so far, we've put you in such a safe little bubble you just never learned how to cope.'

'Uh. What?'

'Alright; that's it.' She grabs a shirt from my closet and tosses it to me on the bed. 'Get dressed.'

'Umm. Okay.' I try to blink the haze away from my eyes. 'Where are we going?'

'*I'm* not going anywhere,' she says. '*You're* going out for a ride with your father.'

* * *

They call it the Oval for a reason, because that's all it is—an oval stretch of road that's closed on weekends for joggers and bikers and families looking for a quick stroll and some fresh air. All things considered, the weather is pretty comfortable, the summer sun not too relentless and the afternoon breeze easing through us, warm and welcoming. Quiet bursts of laughter spring up here and there, friends hanging out and kids running around and babies squealing in delight. A couple of street vendors are stationed a few steps away to my right, peddling buttered corn cobs and sticks of unspeakably sinful delights dipped in fried oil.

The smell alone is making my mouth water. But Dad hasn't brought me here for a picnic. He brought me here to talk.

We're sitting on one of the benches littered on the sidewalks, watching as runners and cyclists zip by.

It's a beautiful day.

'I used to come here all the time.' Dad smiles. 'It's nice to see that some things never change.'

Of course. This is my father's alma mater, and my mother's is a neighbouring university across the same huge street. 'Did you and Mom hang out here all the time?'

'Not your mother, Nat.' He grins. 'Some other girl.'

I stare at him with my mouth hanging open, and he guffaws.

'Relax, son. I'm not having an affair.' He shakes his head, still laughing. 'It was a long time ago, even before I met your mother. She wasn't my first love, you know. There was . . . someone else.'

My jaw is still open. I always thought my parents' relationship is perfect—boy meets girl and girl meets boy and best friends to lovers and firsts-and-lasts. I know I'm in that stage in my life when we're supposed to be all angsty and rebellious, declaring with unquestionable finality that my parents are out to get me and ruin my life and stuff, but I'm not like most of the kids my age. I get along well with the parents. They're pretty cool. Plus, they're the whole reason why I've always believed in love in the first place.

'Same high school, same college, same likes and dislikes. We were inseparable. I thought for sure that I was going to marry her one day, like it was a given, an absolute certainty that was only a question of when,' Dad shrugs. 'But as it turned out, she had . . . other plans, so she left, and she took my plans with her. Life's funny that way, sometimes.

'When I met your mother, I promised myself I would never, ever return to this place again. There were too many memories,

and I didn't trust myself to be over them just yet,' Dad goes on.
'But just a short while into the relationship, your mother took
me here for a quick jog. I couldn't refuse—I could never refuse
her—and so I found myself back here, again, at the place I swore
I'd never return to.

'I was convinced things would go horribly wrong, and in a
way, they did. Barely a few minutes after we started jogging, the
rain started to pour—a sudden, heavy, proper thunderstorm—and
we took shelter under an old bell tower. Right there.' Dad points
to the distance, and I can see a rickety old structure protruding
from afar. 'We thought we could wait out the rain for a bit, but
as the minutes ticked by, the downpour only grew stronger and
stronger, lightning and thunder and floodwater spewing out from
the clogged storm drain on the ground. We knew it was only
going to get worse, so we made the wisest, most horrible decision
ever—we made a run for it.'

'No way.' I'm all in now. 'How far off were you guys?'

'Pretty far.' Dad shakes his head and grins at the memory.
'But we braved the thunderstorm. We ran as fast as we could, our
clothes drenched, our socks soaked with all the floodwater and
our shoes ruined for all eternity.' He laughs. 'We eventually made
it back to the car, which was surrounded by ankle-deep puddles by
then. We sloshed through and barricaded ourselves inside. I was
a hundred percent sure we would catch a cold and die a terrible
death, shivering and stranded.'

'What happened? Did the car get submerged in the flood or
something?'

'I thought it would, so I knew we had to get out of there
as soon as possible. But we couldn't very well just stay inside
drenched to the bones, could we? Luckily for us, we brought a
quick change of clothes we were planning to use after the run.
And because looking for a changing room wasn't an option, we
stripped and changed right there inside the cramped car.'

At my horrified expression, Dad bursts out laughing. 'It was nothing sexual, believe me. Nothing about the whole thing was anything remotely close to romantic,' he says. 'We slipped out of the soaking monstrosities and towelled ourselves dry and slipped right into our dry clothes then drove away from the park and waited out the rain somewhere safe. As soon as we knew we wouldn't drown in the flood any time soon, we stared at each other and couldn't stop laughing. And that was it for me.'

Dad looks up at the trees towering above us, his crinkled eyes smiling at the memory. I look up at the trees too and notice that some of the leaves are too close but aren't touching. Crown shyness, I think it's called, and the thought of it always makes me feel a little sad.

'My point is, Nat, that things don't always turn out the way we want them to,' Dad says, the two of us looking back at each other. 'But the beauty is that sometimes, when our plans backfire, something better and more wonderful comes along that makes everything worthwhile.'

'Thanks, Dad. I like that story.' I sigh. 'I always thought that you and Mom were first loves. She always says you're both lucky enough to have married your best friend.'

'Oh, Nat. Your mother had someone else too before I came along.' Dad smiles at me. 'We didn't *marry* our best friend, son. We became best friends *because* we got married.'

And just like that, my parents effectively shatter all my hopes and dreams and everything I have ever believed about love.

'These things take a lot of work, Nat. Relationships are a tricky thing.' He puts an arm around my shoulder and squeezes. 'I'm just saying that things change; plans change. But that doesn't mean you should be afraid to move on. You can't let your fear paralyse you. You just have to learn how to roll with the punches, you know?'

I stare up some more at the leaves too shy to touch each other, living their lives forever close but forever apart.

"'I was never yours to begin with.'"

'What?'

'Lena. Those were some of the last things she told me before she left.' I look down at the ground. 'I know I'm not supposed to be afraid, but I am. I'm terrified. With last words like those, there's no way to save it all, Dad. I don't think this is something I can fix.'

'Nat. It's not called bravery if you're not scared, you know. Besides, being fearless doesn't mean you should force your wants and needs on the world. Sometimes, being fearless means knowing when to admit you're wrong, too,' Dad says. 'And as for Lena's last words, she was right. You're still thinking about this whole thing as something you can fix, but this isn't one of your games, son. Lena isn't a prize you can win.'

And there it is.

All this time, I have been setting a single-minded goal of starting the game, fighting the Big Boss, and winning the girl.

But it's not a game.

Lena is not a prize. She is a beautiful, vibrant, dynamic human being, capable of making her own decisions, her own paths, and her own dreams, far, far away from me.

She is entitled to do whatever the hell she wants.

And what about me, though? Me and my unchanging life, staying in my own lane and forever afraid to step out of my role. Me as an NPC, with my predetermined mindset and my predetermined lines, standing in the background and going along with the plot. Is this all I want to be?

After a few more minutes of the two of us staring at the people going by and my heart crumpling further and further into itself, Dad clears his throat.

'Alright. What do you say we go get some pizza?'

The idea of my parents falling in love under a thunderstorm amid past heartbreaks hits me harder than ever. 'Maybe in a minute.' My voice breaks. 'Let's stay here for a bit more, Dad. Is that okay?'

'Of course.' My father smiles. 'When you're young, a lot of things may seem like it's the end of the world, but it isn't that bad. Besides, a broken heart is an open heart, right?'

My dad is the smartest person ever, and I'm not even being sarcastic about it.

'You'll be okay, son.' He wraps an arm around me again. 'You'll be okay.'

Twelve

In Which I Look for the Complaint Department and End Up Schooled by the Evil Corporate Overlord

'I've got you now, you oversized koala bear!' I scream at the TV and button-mash like crazy. 'You are *so* going down!'

'Not if I can help it!' Josh leaps from my computer chair. 'You're going *down* down!'

I shoot up along with him, and we both howl like we're crazed and rabid. My character drops dead on-screen just as the huge K.O. sign flashes, and Josh's character—a buff ball of muscle that does look like a koala bear—poses in a triumphant victory stance with my character's spine in his hand. To fully punctuate his gloating, Josh starts dancing around my cramped room.

'Damn it.' I sink back down on my bed. 'I have nothing more to teach you. Except maybe your gaming vernacular. The trash-talking can use some work.'

Josh pumps his controller into the air and whoops. After teaching him all the moves I know all afternoon, I got him to play this mega-violent fighting game he's never been interested in. He's never been interested in video games, to be honest, but right now, with both our hearts ready to burst with all the pent-up *feels*, there's no activity more apt than this.

What was it Lena said? Totally cathartic and totally irresponsible. Yep.

'That felt sooo good.' Josh crashes into my chair. 'Blood and gore. Who would have thought?'

'You're welcome.' I put the game on pause. 'You speak to Bea yet?'

'We actually did get to talk. She cried. I cried. It's still a bad breakup.' Josh shakes his head. 'She will henceforth be referred to as She Who Must Not Be Named.'

'Okay. From a three-letter name to six words. Cool.'

'The heart wants what it wants. But speaking of.' Josh tosses his controller onto the bed. 'There's . . . this girl.'

'Whoa, whoa, whoa.' I sit up straighter. 'There's a girl?'

'Yeah. No. I don't know.' Josh bites his lip. 'It's nothing much, but she's a member of this online forum I'm in. You know, the one I told you about? The comics and stuff? Nothing's happened, but she's pretty cool. So. I dunno.'

'Don't do this to me, man. I need deets.'

'Nothing's happened,' Josh repeats. 'She makes superhero-themed bentos and posts them on her Instagram account. She's funny. And I think she gets me.'

Josh looks down. 'I'm not going to make a move. It's too soon, and I don't want to be a douche. But, you know, maybe someday. One day. Hopefully.'

'That's awesome, Josh.' I grin. 'Superman-sandwich-level awesome.'

'Yeah. Thanks.' He grins back. 'What's up with you and Lena, though? Still giving you the cold shoulder?'

I shrug.

'Look. This may not be what you want to hear right now . . .'

I sigh. 'Here we go.'

'I've said it before, and I'll say it again. You can't be together by default. Love just doesn't work that way.'

'Did you forget she helped you when you were wallowing in self-pity after your breakup?'

'She did, but what you said the day after, about growing together and not outgrowing each other? That helped me more. You've got this friendship thing down.'

'I'm not convinced, but thanks.'

'Take this tough love like a good soldier.' He gestures to my computer monitor. 'I see your essay isn't doing any better, either.'

'It'll come to me.'

'Uh-huh.'

'It will.'

'Sure.'

I stare at Josh, and he stares at me, his wild, curly hair even wilder than his eyes. He has always been that way, wide-eyed and curious and always ready to take anything on. During the first day of pre-school, Mom had made me a Superman sandwich to make me feel super or something, red strawberry jam with the letter 'S' pressed onto the toast, and Josh sat beside me and thought it was the most awesome thing in the world.

So, I split the sandwich with this wild-haired kid who talked to me endlessly about all the capes and cowls, and then he grew up to be this explosively energetic go-getter who joined everything and made friends with everyone. When he told Lena he was the most popular kid in our school, he was not kidding.

Of course, he only ever hangs out with me, cooped up in my room like this like he *chose* me for some reason.

And now that we've just graduated, it's only a matter of time before he realizes all that time he's wasted with me.

'I'm scared.' I blurt out.

'Of what?'

'Of everything changing.'

'Oh. There you go.' Josh tilts his head at me. 'I was wondering when that would come out.'

I let out a long, drawn-out breath. 'I guess I never let myself think about it before, but it's always been there.' Josh took up graphic design at this prestigious university where the tuition fees alone are hella expensive, but I have always had this theory that my best friend is a secret millionaire with all the money he makes doing sponsorships for his unboxing featurettes.

When first semester starts in a few weeks, he'll be a hit. He won't have any problems making new friends over there.

Me, on the other hand . . . I haven't made any real, lasting friendships through the years. Now Josh is leaving. The only thing left that was constant in my life was Lena, and she's leaving too.

'I guess I clung onto the idea of that scholarship because it means something will be certain, at least. That my career path is secure. And that Lena will be right there with me. Now, Lena's just another should-have that I thought was a given. It sucks. I suck. And I handled things horribly.' I shake my head. 'I'm not very good at adapting to this "change" thing.'

I sigh. 'And I know there's this girl you met online and I'm happy for you, but how are you able to do that? How are you able to believe that things will be different this time, even after that horrible breakup? How are you able to find the strength to move on and try again?'

Josh looks up at the ceiling for a bit, then sighs too. 'I don't know. I guess you can call me naïve or something, but I just . . . believe. I mean, I don't know how it'll work out but that doesn't mean it's not worth the risk. It might be awesome. I can't be afraid to try.'

'You know what? Dad told me the exact same thing yesterday.' I grin at him. 'You *do* know things.'

'What did I tell you?' He grins back. 'Mr C knows his stuff too, and I'm glad he's doing okay. And hey, about this "everything is changing" thing, we'll be fine, you and me. I need them Superman sandwiches. It's a bromance thing.'

'Bromance. Right.' I shake my head and we both share a laugh. 'Thanks, I guess.'

'Speaking of sandwiches, I'm starved.' Josh gets up from the chair. 'Lemme see if I can get Mrs C to whip up a nice batch for us.'

The moment he yanks the door open, Mom appears right there in the doorway, looking confused as ever.

'Mrs C!'

'Josh. Hello.' Mom blinks a few times, then turns to me. 'Sweetie, there's . . . someone here for you.'

Josh raises a mock eyebrow at me. 'You got other friends, man?'

'Nope.' I get up from the bed. 'Who is it?'

At this, Mom throws me a weird expression, like she expects a full report about all this right after. 'I think, honey, that you'd better go down and see for yourself.'

* * *

As I slide into the passenger seat of Raf's ultra-smooth, ultra-cool car, I feel the last remnants of my dignity shred themselves away. It's not even a run-down vehicle that reveals serious, deep-seated insecurities and psychological scars. It's just a Rafael Antonio car—something I would expect from a guy who does the mega-heroic voice of noble warrior-god Apolaki.

Whatever's left of my pride promptly scurries away.

With a last wave at his fans, Raf pulls away from the kerb of our shop and turns to me.

'So. Where to?' He dazzles me with his smile. 'Any good places to eat around here?'

The sidewalk grillery immediately pops into my mind, but the thought of Raf sullying what was once mine and Lena's makes me want to hurl. Besides, I should start opening myself up to new things. Maybe give this whole 'change' thing a try.

'There's a new milk tea place not too far from here,' I say. 'It's supposed to be good. Josh waited two hours in the sun for that.'

Raf chuckles. 'Well, if he waited two hours.'

He turns the corner then, looking fresh behind the wheel like he's meant to advertise for a car ad even though he's not even trying.

Just a five-minute drive and we're already here. He parks right up front because a space opens up just for him, the universe never failing to remind me that I'm in the presence of gaming royalty. We walk right in—there's no two-hour line, thankfully—grab our drinks, and find a spot near the counter.

Raf's not being harassed out here. He's only ever a real celebrity in the gaming world, but out here, he's just a regular dude—a regular, super confident, super cool dude.

I give up.

'So, erm.' I clear my throat. 'What's up?'

'You tell me.' Raf throws me a half-smile, like I'm his little brother he just doesn't know how to deal with. 'After the mixer, I had a few meetups lined up for Lena. Just a couple of sound guys I wanted her to learn from. But she never showed.'

I stare down at the milky creaminess of my tea and don't say a word.

'Congratulations, by the way—I was told you kicked ass like a pro back there.' Raf goes on. 'But Lena's ghosted on me, and I have a feeling you had a little something to do with it.'

Something inside me stirs.

'I'm not blaming you or anything. But you're a nice guy, Nat, and this means a lot for Lena's future. You're her best friend. If anything's up, you would know first.'

And it snaps.

'Why do you do it?'

Raf blinks. 'Excuse me?'

'This. This whole act of helping Lena with her future and shit. Why do you do it?' I grit my teeth. 'Do you like her? Because you might as well come out and say it. You like her, you always have, and let's be honest, because Lena's awesome and you'd be stupid not to like her. So just say it, and maybe I'll hate you less.'

Raf is silent for a beat, two beats, three. In those three seconds that stretch out into infinity, I feel like I have gone and doomed myself, and I will probably get punched in the face by one of the most important people in the corporate gaming industry and be banned from Tala Tales Games and *Mitolohiya* forever.

I clench my fist to keep from trembling. But then Raf smiles. Then he shakes his head. Then he laughs.

And now *I* want to punch him in the face.

'Nat. If you think that I like Lena, you're right.'

My heart drops.

'And she *is* awesome. She is skilled and funny and passionate and smart. Which is why I see a lot of potential in her. In her future. And I know she'll go far.'

'Okay,' I mutter. Now that he has actually gone ahead and said it, it just makes me feel much, much worse. I don't even know what to say or do next.

'So yeah, man, I like her. But as for you hating me, you shouldn't.' Raf shrugs. 'I have a girlfriend. Lena's too young for me.'

Oh.

Oh.

Now I feel like a complete jerk.

'So,' Raf takes a quick sip of his milk tea, still smiling that incredibly gracious smile. 'You like Lena, huh?'

I burn up. 'Umm—'

He throws me a teasing smirk. 'She likes you too, you know. She always has.'

What.

'But the thing is, she likes sound mixing too,' he goes on. 'And if you truly cared about her, you wouldn't want her to have to choose between the two of you, would you?'

My heart constricts, because he's right.

Rafael Antonio is right.

It doesn't make me hate him less.

'I'm sorry,' I blurt out, 'for saying I hate you and stuff. Um. You don't deserve it.'

'You're too nice, Nat. If I were in your shoes, I would've socked myself ages ago.' He laughs. 'You need to learn to loosen up a little though, yeah? Be more flexible. Learn to adapt. After all, you can't keep using the same moves over and over again in any strategy game, right? Same goes for life, I'm afraid. You just have to go with it sometimes.'

People have told me this over and over again for the past two days. I'm starting to think the universe is out to get me.

'Can I give you a piece of advice?'

Haven't you been schooling me enough already? 'Sure.'

'I can't claim to be an expert in relationships, so how you deal with your feelings for Lena is your thing. But I do know this—whatever happens, the least you can do is support your friends. Help them pursue their dreams. Be there for them and encourage them, even if that means them being apart from you.' Raf looks down, and for the first time since I met him, I see a hint of vulnerability in his eyes. 'When you go big on your dreams, not everyone is going to stick around. So, when someone does . . . well, that's a keeper.'

Sticking around . . . supporting Lena's dreams . . . I should've been doing that from the start. Instead, I've been so caught up in keeping things the same that I went and ruined the best thing that's ever happened to me, all because I've been too afraid to change.

I've been treating Raf as the Big Boss Fight I need to defeat in this game of life, but as it turns out, I'm the boss fight. I'm my own arch-nemesis. I'm the villain who keeps standing in the way.

So, I offer my olive branch. 'Thanks, Raf. For everything. And I'm sorry.'

'Hey, I haven't done anything. And I'm not the one you should be apologizing to. But for what it's worth, though, I hope you do get that scholarship. It'll be nice to see a friendly face at HQ whenever I need some voice work done.' He claps me on the back. 'You're a good guy, Nat. You'll figure this out.'

I smile at him, and he grins back.

'Actually, Raf, I wonder if I could ask you a favour . . .'

* * *

I offer a polite little nod at the technician beside me, who touches a finger to his lips to remind me for the hundredth time to stay silent.

I'm hiding in the shadows on the other side of the sound booth, where the magic of music is happening at the moment. Random outsiders aren't normally allowed to sit in on recording sessions like this, but with Raf working his charm around everyone at HQ, I've been allowed to squeeze in behind the scenes.

Raf is somewhere in the building, though. He's not recording anything—in fact, he's already done with his voice work for Apolaki in the expansion pack. There are no new developments surrounding *Mitolohiya* at the moment, so he hasn't been coming in to work much lately.

But he's not the one I'm here to see.

On the other side of the recording booth, Lena emerges, all hyped up and ready to go. Just like her prepping for her matches, here is how her first few minutes go:

1. She licks her lips.
2. Her eye twitches.
3. She cracks her neck to the left, then to the right.

But contrary to any *Mitolohiya* match, I know nothing about what any of this means.

For the first time ever, I'm clueless about Lena's life. This is a whole other side of her, a great big unknown, a territory beyond the bounds of anything she has ever shared with me. And I know nothing about this part of her world.

When everyone is ready, she poises her fingers over the console in front of her, and she plays.

She plays her music.

A haunting melody comes on, filled with all the ebbs and flows I know she is capable of, the rise and fall and all the feels that always blow me away. This is her demo reel, the mix she has been working on, the one that Raf got her a chance to showcase, her passion, her one true dream.

I look around at everyone in the sound booth, and there is not a single face that isn't spellbound, not a single soul Lena hasn't captured with her sound.

My heart swells with so much pride that my eyes water.

When her demo is over, the people over on her end start chatting animatedly with her with smiles on their faces. I can't make out what they're saying, but even though I can see that Lena's a wreck, it's a good wreck. She's nervous and edgy and just so, so happy.

The technician beside me gives me a small nudge then. 'Aren't you going over there?'

I came here because I wanted to apologize, but seeing her now doing her thing, I don't think her seeing me here will do her any good.

'No, I . . . I should go. Thank you so much for your time.'

'Your friend's got something there, kid,' the technician says before I head out the door. 'You oughta be happy for her.'

I look at Lena from afar one last time, blissful and content, like she is totally in her element, like she has finally found where she belongs, like she is finally home.

'Yeah.' I smile. 'I am.'

Thirteen

In Which I Reset My Stats and Reroll

Tala Tales Games HQ looks different to me now, like the very same walls and halls are bigger somehow. Strolling down the office like this, outside of tour hours and with no Lena in sight, it's like stepping into a different world I never noticed before. Everything from the bright art deco to the plain ol' carpet seems to have changed since the last time I was here—or, maybe, I'm the one who's changed.

The guys and gals pulling an all-nighter are still in that same spot I saw them in, though. Laptops are open, notes are strewn about, and there's no shortage of snacks, coffee cups, and empty bottles of carbonated drinks littered across their desks. I stop just outside the room, staring at them through the glass walls like they're on display. I wish I could hear what they're doing in there.

'Hey, kiddo!'

A cheery voice chirps to my left and breaks my trance. Orange Hoodie Dude is walking down the hall toward me, that perpetually bubbly mod who looks like he has one of the coolest jobs in the world, and maybe he does. He is still wearing the same hoodie.

'You're from the summer scholarship programme, right?' he says when he is right beside me. 'No tours today, I'm afraid. Did you get your schedule mixed up?'

'Umm, no. I just felt like dropping by before the essay is due tomorrow.' I scratch the back of my neck. 'I guess I don't know why I'm here, either.'

'Ah. Getting a feel of your future here, are ya?' He beams. 'I'll be straight with you, kid. This is the coolest place I've ever worked in—the energy and creativity are just off the charts. I'm not even kidding.'

'You don't need to tell me twice.' I smile at him. 'Do you mind if I ask what's going on in that room?'

'Not at all.' He shakes his head. 'That, my friend, is a hackathon.'

'A what?'

'A hackathon. It's a 24-hour challenge where programmers and software designers work together to develop something in a short amount of time.' He nods his head at the people in the room. 'Participants can come out of the event with a prototype or something complete and good to go, but essentially, it's collaborative coding at its finest.'

'Whoa. A working prototype in just twenty-four hours?'

'Sometimes a weekend. Depends on the event.'

'Whoa,' I repeat. Upon closer inspection, what I thought was the same group of people I saw last time turns out to be a different set, but still with the same spark of determination in their tired but happy eyes.

'It's a great way to gain industry experience, meet like-minded individuals, and, of course, nab cash prizes. Pretty cool, huh?'

'*Very* cool.' I nod. 'Does that happen here often at HQ?'

'More frequently lately than they were before. The industry is ever-changing, and it's exhilarating.'

'Did you ever participate in one? A hackathon?'

'Me?' He waves his hands in front of him and laughs. 'I'm not a programmer. All I know is basic code. I moderate the tours because I'm in PR.'

That makes sense. He is one of the happiest people I have ever met.

'I get in touch with game journos who work with us to write pieces on our games. And they're not just reviews and press releases—the journalists can write guides and tips for our games too, which is a huge thing for our mobile apps, especially.'

'The *Mitolohiya* spin-off isn't the only thing going mobile?'

'Definitely not. While *Mitolohiya* is huge right now, we can't rely on a single franchise to survive. We have to know how to adapt to a fast-paced industry and invest as much TLC into mobile too, for both hardcore and casual gamers across the globe. It's exciting, isn't it?'

Somehow, without my misguided mission constantly fogging up my thoughts and clouding my vision, I can see and think more clearly about what I want to do.

And yes, it is everything Orange Hoodie Dude just said.

'You know, you kind of remind me of my younger sister. Used to baulk at anything programming-related, but she got a taste of programming during a career talk in high school and never looked back.' He shrugs, and I can't believe my weird, random impression about him was actually right when I first saw his 'Girl Gamers Rock' lanyard. 'Around your age too, I'd say.'

'Must be cool to work in the same company.'

'Her? Here? God, no.' He laughs. 'That doofus specifically *chose* to compete against me. After college, she's got her heart set on working for a rival company to get under my skin. Says she's going to be the greatest programmer in the world.'

I smile. 'Sounds like a pretty cool sister.'

He smiles back. 'Guess I shouldn't be saying this, but my point is that you could work somewhere else too, if you wanted to. Don't, though. This place is the best.'

'Thank you,' I say. 'I can't believe I'm saying this, but I wish I tried harder throughout the programme. It just feels like not getting in is not an option anymore.'

'The scholarship isn't your only chance, kid.' Orange Hoodie Dude winks. 'There are many different paths to a game's success.

We all work toward the same goal, but there are tons of different ways to get there.'

With everything I have learned about life this week, I have a feeling that this concept definitely doesn't apply solely to game dev.

* * *

I clutch the printout tighter in my hand and swallow for the hundredth time. When I hit 'Send' on that submission email a while back, I printed out a copy and stuffed it in a nice little envelope with Lena's name scribbled on the back. She has been avoiding me like the plague lately, but it gave me enough reason to type up my essay like I'm on steroids.

Everything just flowed right through me then, the thoughts and the feelings and everything that, looking back, I probably shouldn't have word-vomited on a scholarship application essay. But it's there now, floating through cyberspace on the way to Tala Tales Games HQ, and after reading and re-reading it for the millionth time, I think it's the best way I can maybe get Lena to talk to me again.

At this point, after detoxifying my own stupidity, all I want now is for Lena to forgive me. It's not even about my unrequited feelings—I'm way past that now. I just want her to know that I'll support her all the way, and that I can still be her friend—if she'll accept me.

Maybe.

Hopefully.

Jury is still out on that one.

Which is why I've been standing out here at their front porch for who-knows-how-long, squirming and fidgeting and unable to ring the doorbell. Because if she's not home and *Ate* Ami answers the door, I'd die on the spot.

But if she *is* home and *she* answers the door, I'd die on the spot, too.

You got this, Nat. I take a deep breath. *It's just an essay. No biggie. Just a piece of paper with all my feelings in it and the possibility of getting a scholarship or ruining my future or losing Lena forever hanging in the balance. Just that. No big deal.*

I grit my teeth, clear my throat, and ring the doorbell.

And Lena's father answers the door.

Crap.

He furrows his brows at me, his eyes slowly, slowly trying to register who I am and what the hell a scrawny little teenage boy is doing trembling on his doorstep.

'Umm. Hi, Mr Dizon. Umm. Is Lena there?'

'She's out,' he drawls.

'Oh. Okay.' I stay there and freeze. This is *not* going well.

Thankfully, Mr Dizon frowns at me even more. 'Nat?'

'Yeah. Yes! I mean, yes, Mr Dizon, it's me, Nat. Lena's friend.' It's now or never. 'Could you, umm . . . could you maybe please give this to Lena for me?'

I hand him the neat little envelope with Lena's name on it, and he stares at it for the longest two seconds ever. I feel like I'm watching him in slow motion, like he's one of those cartoon sloths on TV, the ones that take forever just to get a word out.

'Sure,' he manages to say.

'Thank you, sir.' I hesitate. 'That's all. I . . . I should go. I'm sorry to bother you during your . . . rest.'

He stares at me, expressionless, with the unkempt beard and the messy hair and the clothes that look like he has been sleeping in them for days. Then he manages a small smile at me, as he wipes something moist around the corner of an eye.

'Thank you for the movies. You're a good kid, Nat,' he says. 'You're a good kid.'

He turns around and shuts the door behind him.

So.

What the hell do I do now?

I spin around and walk back down the street away from the Dizons' house, when the front door bursts open behind me, and I hear footsteps running toward my direction.

'Nat! Nat!'

My heart surges at the split-second thought that Lena might be running toward me, ready to forgive me for being the biggest jerk in the history of all jerks, but I know I'm not that lucky. I turn around, and it's *Ate* Ami.

'Hey,' she pants out my name and skids to a stop in front of me.

I give her a moment to catch her breath. 'Hi, *Ate* Ami.'

She waves my unopened letter in front of my face. 'What's all this?'

'It's . . . just my scholarship essay.' I go red. 'I was hoping Lena would read it.'

'An essay.' *Ate* Ami raises an eyebrow. 'You're trying to reach Lena with an essay?'

'Yeah.' I place a hand behind my neck. 'We're not exactly on speaking terms right now.'

'Nat.' *Ate* Ami sighs. 'You do know that she's a real person, right?'

She shakes her head. 'Listen. I know all about what happened at the mixer, and as protective as I am of Lena, I can't say I'm 100 percent mad at you. I know what it's like to be young and in love, and to have absolutely no clue what to do about it.'

'Um . . .'

'I also know what it's like to be scared of the Big Bad Future, to not know which path to take from here. So, I'm going to tell you the same thing I told Lena when she mustered up the courage to confront me about her sound mixing—be your best self.'

She pauses for effect, and for a second I recognize that spark of stubborn determination in her eye that mirrors Lena's perfectly.

'Be your best self. That's it,' *Ate* Ami repeats. 'You can do what your parents want you to do, what society tells you to do, or what your heart tells you to do. You *can* choose. You *can* make mistakes. You *can* start over. Life is hard enough on you already— you don't have to be so hard on yourself, too.'

I'm reeling.

'When our mom left us, I *chose* this responsibility, Nat. It wasn't my dream, but I chose this, taking care of Lena and our father. And I like what I do. I'm damn good at it, and I have no regrets,' she goes on. 'With Lena, and with you, the possibilities are endless. You both don't have to be torn between doing what you *want* to do and doing what you *need* to do. They don't have to be polar opposites, you know?'

'*Ate* Ami . . .'

She shakes her head again and cuts me off. 'I've said my piece. Now. I'm still going to give Lena this essay of yours, but it's not an apology, Nat. It's a piece of paper. It's no substitute for the real you.'

And with that, she waves the envelope at me and turns back toward their house.

Now all I have to do is wait.

Fourteen

In Which Rage-Quitting is Not an Option

What motivates you? By Nathaniel Carpio

Fear. Fear is what motivates me. I know that sounds horrible, because how can anyone be driven by fear? How can anyone be happy being afraid all the time? But I have come to realize a few things over the summer, and that's just the thing—I really am afraid.

I'm afraid of things changing. Of not knowing what the future holds for me, of what might happen in my career or my future or my life. Everyone always tells the youth that the world is our oyster, that we've got our whole lives ahead of us, that we can go out and conquer the world and dream big. But it's not that simple, is it? The future is big and scary and uncertain and full of failures, and when you've got that kind of endless possibility ahead of you, it's impossible not to get overwhelmed.

The thing is, I'm always scared. I'm scared of making the wrong decisions, of letting people down, of losing the ones who are most important to me. I'm scared of a lot of things, but I learned something else over the summer too. I learned that it's okay to feel fear—what matters more is how I react to that fear.

If I'm afraid of failing, then I should do everything I can to strive for success. If I'm afraid of losing, then I should train and learn from mistakes and adapt to win. If I'm afraid of what the future holds, of losing friends and changing paths and going separate ways, then I should do my best to accept change as it is. It's not about doing whatever it takes to make sure things stay the same. It's about adapting, learning, and growing to be a better person.

It's all about embracing the change. Gaining experience points. Levelling up. After all, I am not an NPC. A non-playable character doesn't level up. It stays the same, day in and day out, as adventurers and heroes and villains come and go with every playthrough. I used to think that's what I wanted—to keep things the same, to go through the motions so I wouldn't have to face the uncertainty of the future, the fear of that great big unknown.

But I am not an NPC. I refuse to be one.

It's not easy—not even a little bit. Change is constant, especially in this industry. But because of this, there's nothing we can do but make each moment count, right? Be with the people we love, support them, be there for them. Enjoy each second, laugh when we can, be kind. While there's nothing we can do to stop the flow of time, there is something we can do to make time worthwhile—we can love.

I was told once that there is no fear in love, but maybe that's not the point. Maybe the point is that fear is always there, but it's just that love sort of overcomes it, you know? It may still be there, the pain and the suffering, but love helps you make it through to the other side. It doesn't promise you'll be unscathed, but you'll be okay; you'll be okay.

So yes, it's the fear that keeps me going. But out of that fear, I've come to learn about life and love and family and friends, and that ultimately—ultimately—all I need to win in this game of life is not just to go from start to finish but to enjoy the little in-betweens, the side quests and the treasure chests and the pleasant Easter eggs, and maybe come out of it all saying, 'Good game.'

After all, the gameplay is really what it's all about, isn't it?

'Write your name down and sign here, please.' I slide the registration sheet across the long table. 'Once you pay for the fee, you'll get a unit assigned to you.'

'Thanks,' a guy with a *Mitolohiya* cap answers, bending down to scribble his signature on the sheet of paper. He hands it back to me and shuffles along toward my mother, who is in charge of collecting payments over at the counter.

I turn to the next guy in line at the makeshift registration area Josh and I are handling, a long table with sign-up sheets and two of us seated behind it in Monobloc chairs. It's a humid morning, the air just ripe enough for a good ol' online competition. The turnout's not so bad, actually—there's a line that snakes out onto the sidewalk as players sign up for a chance to prove their prowess, bag the cash prize, and get dubbed as the ultimate *Mitolohiya* champion—at least for the next couple of hours after the competition ends.

Dad is busy zipping across the shop making last-minute preparations at the gaming stations, and thankfully, Josh volunteered his time out here today to keep me company and help with the clean-up after. Even Raf was nice enough to send out a few boxes of autographed Apolaki posters this morning, something we can definitely use as an added perk for anyone who signs up.

Plus, Dad has been obsessing about this event the whole summer. I want this to work for his sake.

'Write your name down and sign here, please.' I repeat without looking up, as the person next in line walks up to our table. 'Once you pay for the fee, you'll get a unit assigned to you.'

The person doesn't reply, and I feel Josh tense up beside me. I look up from the sheet.

Lena is standing there in a white tank top, her long hair gathered in a fuss-free braid behind her like she's ready to kick some ass.

Then, she smiles.

I realize how much I have built her up in my head after not seeing her for the longest time and how anyone can be that beautiful, but she is, she is, and she's right here, and she's even more radiant than I ever could have imagined.

'Just sign right here?' She asks with a playful tilt of her head like she's teasing me.

'Uh, yeah.' I tap on the next line on the registration sheet. 'Just . . . here.'

'Got it.' She bends down and scribbles her name. I'm still in complete shock, so Josh clears his throat and redeems myself for me.

'Thanks, Lena of the Land of Lamenting Thumbs.' Josh cocks his head over to my mom with a grin. 'Just pay for the fee over there by Mrs C and you're good to go.'

'No biggie.' She winks at Josh. 'Wish me luck, yeah?'

'You won't need it!' Josh calls out after her as she moves on to the counter. When she's properly out of earshot, Josh nudges me with his elbow, hard.

'What's wrong with you, man? Snap out of it.'

'R-right. Sorry.' I shake my head. 'I just . . . she . . . how am I—'

'Uh, hello?' The girl next in line crosses her arms over her chest, scowling at us. 'Am I supposed to sign here or what?'

'I got this.' Josh pushes me out of my chair. 'You go straighten yourself out.'

'Umm. Okay.'

I leave Josh at the station for a while and head out the back exit of the shop. I lean against the wall and take a deep breath.

Lena's here. She's signed up for the competition and she's making an appearance and has she read the essay, has she forgiven me, does she think I'm an ass, and do I look okay?

I close my eyes and breathe. Lena is here, but it's competition day. It's all about the event Dad's been stressing over for the past weeks, and I need to focus on that.

This whole thing with Lena is just gonna have to wait.

When I feel like I am back to being a fully functional human being, I step back inside.

Even amid the sea of people crammed inside the shop, Lena still stands out from the crowd in my eyes, like there's this ray of light shining down from above that only I can see. I look around and Mom catches my eye. Even Dad stops fussing about for a second to throw me a reassuring look.

I smile. With a support group like this, I can do anything.

* * *

It's over. Temper tantrums, free Apolaki posters, and a great deal of trash-talking later, the competition is over, with some kid from a few blocks down winning the overall championship. A few of the contestants did some major rage-quitting along the way, and Lena made it to the top five without breaking a sweat. But there is always a better player out there, and in the end, the grand prize went to someone else.

Still, beaming and glowing and elated, Lena walks up to both my parents after the match, congratulating them on an awesome turnout and asking Dad how his knee is doing.

I'm sweeping the floor down the aisle when Josh thanks the last customer and shuts the door. There's nobody left inside now except for the four of us, plus Lena.

Lena is still here.

Josh throws me a what-the-hell-are-you-doing look and nods at Lena, still chatting animatedly to my parents by the counter. I hold up my broom to him and shake my head.

He rolls his eyes. 'Hey, Mrs C, you need me to sweep up in here?' He calls out to catch my mother's attention. 'The place is a mess, but I'd be happy to lend my expert services for a bit longer. Just a couple of Superman sandwiches and we can call it even.'

Mom catches on with lightning-quick speed. 'Throw in shutting down all the units, and *then* we'll call it even.' She grins, then turns to me. 'Nat, honey, why don't you walk Lena home today?'

'Yes, son, you should walk Lena home.' Dad pipes in. 'We'll close up in here, so you won't have to worry about a thing.'

Children. I am dealing with children.

'That'll be nice,' Lena says. 'It's been a while, hasn't it, Nat?'

'Umm. Yeah.' I burn up. Josh yanks the broom from me as Mom and Dad blabber on and on about the weather and the humidity and the neighbourhood and me needing to walk Lena home, even though our neighbourhood is perfectly safe, and they have never been concerned about Lena walking home alone before. Then, they lovingly shoo us both outside the shop, still going on and on about the weather, terrible actors trying to deliver their terrible lines.

And just like that, we are alone again, Lena and I, after ages and ages apart.

'So.' I shove my hands into my pockets. 'Hi.'

'Hi.' Lena smiles, and out here in broad daylight, I notice that she's got a few subtle highlights in her hair now, shades of light brown streaked across her braid. 'It's still pretty early to go home. You wanna head to the grillery?'

'We'll suffocate in this heat,' I say. 'How about that milk tea place instead?'

'Sure.' Lena gives me a look of pleasant surprise. 'You've been?'

'Yeah. For a change.' I rub a hand on my nape. 'With Raf, actually.'

'*With Raf?*' Lena's eyes widen. 'Look at you, Nathaniel Carpio. We haven't even started college yet, and you're making new friends already.'

'I know, right?' I smile. 'He's . . . pretty cool.'

Lena returns the smile, and I take a moment to capture the light dancing in her eyes.

We head down the sidewalk we both know so well. It rained for a bit, apparently, when Dad's tournament was going on. Wet puddles are scattered here and there, reflecting my awkwardness right back up at me.

I thought being apart from Lena would gradually ease me into her absence, but seeing her again after so long only makes the pain and the longing much, much worse.

'I saw you, you know.'

'What?'

'At HQ. At my demo. Your ninja moves aren't as effective as you might think. You're no Sigbin.'

'Oh. I'm so sorry. I never meant—'

She shakes her head again, and I don't say anything else about that.

'How are you, Nat?'

I keep my hands inside my pockets. 'Okay. I lost the scholarship.'

'What?' Lena turns to me. 'How is that possible?'

'I was slacking off on the coding assignments, and the game concept proposals I've been writing were way off. As it turns out, I didn't understand the assignment properly. Plus, why I thought I could cruise by with just my *Mitolohiya* skills is beyond me.'

'That sucks.' Lena grumbles. 'What are you going to do now?'

I look up at the sky for a bit, fiery and burning right after the rain. 'I'll still take up programming, then apply to Tala Tales Games again after graduation. I've also been working hard at the shop lately, to ease things a little bit for the folks. Guess I'll just have to see where it goes.'

'No definite plan, huh?'

'No definite plan,' I say. 'You inspired me. To go chase my dreams, but at the same time be more considerate of my family's dreams.'

'Come on, Nat. I can't possibly be an inspiration for anyone.'

'But you are.' My voice grows softer. 'You are to me.'

We walk along in silence again, then I stop in my tracks.

'Lena, I'm sorry.'

She stops too.

'I'm sorry for being stupid and mean and selfish, and for thinking only of myself throughout this whole thing,' I blurt out, realizing that once the words start pouring, it's hard to stop. 'I'm sorry for never considering how you feel, what you want, and how you're struggling inside too. I'm sorry for unloading all my feelings for you at the wrong place and the wrong time, for being insanely jealous and for not even seeing your worth. I'm sorry for not telling you how I feel sooner, for thinking I'm entitled to your feelings just because I've been here all along.'

Lena opens her mouth to speak, but I hold my hands up between us and go on.

'I'm sorry for being so afraid of losing you that I kept all these to myself, but you're right, and I was unfair to you, and I was a shitty friend for not thinking about you first. I had this romanticized idea of you and me in my head, but I was only seeing what I wanted to see,' I say. 'All this time, I've been blindly trying to win you over, but you're not a prize, Lena. And I have absolutely no control over how you want to live your life, with or without my confession.

'I want you to know that I fully support you and your dreams. If you want to be an audio engineer then that would be the coolest thing in the world, because you're you and you can do anything, and I'm not going to let my own stupidity stand in your way, not anymore. I'm sorry.'

I finally run out.

The sun is beginning to set. Wild bursts of orange and blue scatter across the sky, the fading light framing Lena's face from behind like a halo. For a moment, I fear she's going to disappear, like she's just an apparition, the ghost of her smile forever embedded in my mind and the wisps of her forgiveness forever out of reach.

But then she nestles her hand in mine.

'I like you too, you big, stupid idiot. You're the nicest, most annoying, most stubborn guy I have ever met—and yes, I said "guy"'. Her eyes water, but she smiles. 'I've always liked you, which is why I've always felt guilty about spending less and less time with you lately. And it's not like I haven't thought about it, you and me. But I knew I had to focus on myself first, you know? Dad is so lost, and *Ate* Ami's worked so hard, and I just . . .'

'That selfie we took on my birthday. I revisit that picture over and over again, and it breaks my heart to see that look on your face, the way you look at me like I can do no wrong.' She looks down. 'You do that all the time. It terrifies me. You look at me, and the pain is a physical thing. You get this crease between your eyebrows, and I . . . I can't stand it. I can't stand how anyone can hurt you like that, but the worst part is that it's me.'

Her voice breaks, but I'm a mess too. 'When we fought, I took that time to re-align my priorities, to get back on track. I thought about what you said too, about Raf helping me get a foot in the door. I didn't want that. I didn't want any handouts for the motherless girl. I wanted my successes to be judged on my own merits. I wanted to prove to everyone—myself, mostly—that I can do what I want and be damn good at it. Deep down, I wanted to prove to my mother too that I'm doing perfectly fine without her, just out of spite.'

Lena strains to keep her composure. 'Despite his condition, I love Dad so damn much, and I always thought I could never forgive my mother for leaving us. But *Ate* Ami told me a lot of things. She told me it's okay to ask for help from Raf. She even told me that maybe it's a good idea to start seeing Mom again on a regular basis, because all this hatred is going to eat me up. She also told me that if I wanted to be fair to you, I should tell you how I feel, so I am.'

She takes a deep breath. 'That night in my room before the mixer—it was a moment of weakness. I wanted a lot of things that night, but right now, I need to focus on my career and getting good grades and helping out in the house. I just can't afford to fall in love with you, Nat. I won't allow myself to.'

The world stops.

'You mean so much to me, Nat. But my future means a whole lot more.'

I squeeze her hand as tightly as I can. The pain is still there, but this is it—this is my final boss battle, the last stage I have to overcome before it all ends. And since I'm the Big Boss, this is my one, last chance to not be that selfish jerk I have been all this time.

So, I execute the final blow. 'You're right, Lena.' And the evil Big Boss goes down.

'You should go do what you love. Now that I've knocked some long overdue sense into me, it's all so, so clear from the very beginning. You were meant to be an audio engineer.'

Everything snowballs. I hate my voice for shaking so damn much. 'You're one of the most talented, most driven people I know, and I'm not just saying that. You're amazing at what you do, Lena. So please. Go out and chase your dreams. You deserve the world, and there's nothing else you should focus on but to follow your heart. Absolutely nothing or no one else.'

And with that, I let her hand go.

I let Lena go.

Because that is what she deserves.

She deserves a life full of happiness and ambition and fulfilment, of lifelong dreams and never-ending music. She deserves joy and beauty and wonder, practising her passion and basking in her element. She deserves a whole new world out there that is just hers for the taking.

She deserves to be free—and more importantly—because she *wants* to be. That choice has nothing at all to do with me. She doesn't *need* my permission. She doesn't need *me*.

And I should be okay with that.

I am going to be okay.

Nothing and everything happen to me at once. The memory of rain, the longing for old times. The willingness to forget the pain and the stupidity to try again. The times I felt alone even when surrounded by people, the fake confidence, the tiresome façade. The image of me crying in the silence of my room, and the anger and frustration of desperately trying to scrub the tears clean. Moments so spectacular I can still see them, still feel them, still believe that we were happy once.

Like all heartbreaks, Lena is a storm.

And like in all heartbreaks, I will never be the same again.

And then I see it all.

Our sidewalk grillery, the spot we own from the rest of the world, those barbecue stains and training sessions at night, a squeeze on my shoulder, Lena's kiss on my cheek. The milk teas and memories, the trips to the mall and the siomai at the train station during sunset. The online auction and my Bathala agimat. Lena's matching puzzle pieces.

Co-ops for life.

Just co-ops.

Nothing more.

'We're still co-ops, right?' She sniffles.

'Always.'

'That's one of the things I like about you, Nat. You just never know when to rage-quit.' She wipes her nose with the back of her other hand. 'So. How about that milk tea now?'

I take her hand as a friend, surer now than I ever was all these years. 'Milk tea it is, and maybe some chicken inasal after.

I owe my teacher a week's worth, and we wouldn't want Dizon the Devourer to pop up, would we?'

'No.' She beams, squeezing my hand right back. 'We wouldn't.'

* * *

Public. Static. Print. Squiggly Line.

That night in my room, I stare at the 'Hello World' code I hastily jotted down in my notebook what seems like ages and ages ago, still confused but oddly intrigued. There are no *Mitolohiya* matches now, no scholarships on the line, no girl I have been putting on a pedestal for the past years of my life. It's just me and this code—this simple, meaningful, two-liner of a code—holding the beginning and the end in just a handful of words that wouldn't make sense to anyone else.

I open up the online Java compiler on my computer, and— after a deep breath—I start typing.

```
public static void main(String[] args) {
    System.out.println("Hello World!");
}
```

The two words pop up on my screen, bright and happy and filled with so many overwhelming and exciting possibilities, and for some weird reason, my heart swells.

Staring at the 'Hello World!' text on my computer with nothing else and no one else around, I suddenly feel like the whole world has just opened up to me.

Epilogue

In Which the Boss Fight Level
Has a Bonus Stage IRL

My first week on campus will always be defined by three things: getting lost in the labyrinth between the cafeteria and Acosta Hall, signing up for the Much Dev Such Wow club, and getting summoned to the Dean's office before I even knew where the Dean's office was.

I have no idea how I can be in trouble already when I don't even know what counts as trouble yet. But I guess there's no escaping it. So here I am, shuffling my feet and tugging at my campus lanyard for fifteen minutes now. The waiting area isn't that big—just a two-seater sofa with cracked leather that kind of makes it seem like students have been coming in and sitting here to await their doom since the '20s. The secretary's desk is what hogs the whole place, but she's not here, and there's some kind of commotion beyond the closed door to the desk's left, which is where I assume I'll face my doom pretty soon too.

And just when I think I can't fidget any more than I already am, the door bursts open and a harried girl with big, bright, charcoal eyes glares at me. I open my mouth but nothing comes out, so she hurries behind the desk and starts rummaging around in a frenzy, promptly rendering me non-existent.

I gulp. She might just be the Dean's secretary, and whatever they were fussing about just a moment ago probably wasn't about her getting a raise. But I've been delaying my demise for close to half an hour now, so I might as well rip the Band-Aid off and get it over with. So much for that perfect record—and I wanted to impress Tala Tales Games with my stats too, when I apply for a job four years from now.

Taking a deep enough breath that I almost choke from the fake pine scent of the oil diffuser in the room, I march up to the secretary's desk.

'Hello. I'm Nathaniel Carpio.'

The girl continues to act like I'm not there, even as I'm already leaning over the desk so near her crouched form.

'I'm supposed to see Dean Santos today?'

She doesn't seem to be getting anywhere with her search, flipping files and rummaging through the drawers. She gets down on all fours then, squinting under the chair and fanning her hands out across the dingy floor.

'Umm. Hi?'

At this, she heaves a sigh, then flits her eyes up at me so abruptly I thought she would fling me across the room with a stare. 'What?'

'Uh, I'm Nat. Nathaniel?'

'Okay, good for you.'

'Dean Santos said—'

'That's great.' She scratches at a spot near her ear, and I notice she's got one of those short, short haircuts that remind me of a younger Morena Baccarin. A pixie cut, was it called? Yeah. A pixie cut.

It's cute.

'So, uh, do I just head inside, or—'

'Elle!'

The two of us turn to the Dean's office, and there, standing by the doorway with her hands on her hips and a sigh on her lips, s the Dean's actual secretary. I can tell because of the employee ID pinned to her chest and the professional vibe she's giving off right now, much less devil-may-care than my would-be impostor and much more sinister than I'd hoped.

But if she's the Dean's secretary, who's this girl that's been giving me the evil eye this whole time?

'Mrs Rodriguez!' The girl called 'Elle' does a complete 180 and flashes the older woman a blinding smile—sure, she's nice to her, but with me, she's . . . she's . . . what did I do to her, exactly?

'I'm *so* sorry for the mess, but my ID is missing. Since I'm here all the time, you must've stashed it here at your desk somewhere, right?' Elle bats her eyelashes at Mrs Rodriguez, who doesn't seem at all amused that some kid just went through her personal things.

But rather than chastise her like I thought she would, Mrs Rodriguez rolls her eyes, sighs like she doesn't know what to do with Elle, and shoos her out from behind her desk. 'If you've lost your ID *again*, Elle, it's not going to be behind my desk. And it's certainly not going to be my problem.'

'Sorry,' Elle mumbles, stepping beside me now in front of Mrs Rodriguez's desk, but still acting like I'm not there. 'I've got a super important flash drive on that lanyard, and Dean Santos will kill me if I lost that thing. Again.'

Mrs Rodriguez shakes her head. 'You're a smart girl, Elle. You'll figure it out. And mind you, the Dean is not a murderer. But he might just hire someone else to do the dirty job for him.'

Elle bites back a smile, and I suddenly feel like this girl has been part of this tight-knit little circle for the longest time and that I am out of place and intruding. Which is why I try to avert my eyes somewhere else, and they inadvertently land on the couch I was just sitting on a moment ago.

And there, wedged underneath the sofa and sticking out with a hint of bright neon pink, is something that looks like a lanyard.

Elle and Mrs Rodriguez keep talking and I keep walking and then I crouch down and tug at the pink thing on the ground. True enough, it's a lanyard with a flash drive and a student ID hanging from it.

And it's a lanyard I've seen before.

Girl Gamers Rock.

My jaw drops.

'You found it!' A voice booms so loud right behind me that I almost trip while crouched on the ground.

Elle unceremoniously bends down and snatches the lanyard from my hands. 'You rock, dude! Thank you.' She wears it over her head, and I get up from the ground and I still can't believe fate is toying with me right now. It's the same pink lanyard Orange Hoodie Dude was wearing during the summer programme at Tala Tales Games.

Girl Gamers Rock.

'Listen, sorry I was so bitchy back there. It's just—I was busy, you know? And you were standing there acting all weird.' *I was* weird? 'Since you found it, I'll let you in on some top-secret info. This thing has all the files for the Dean's special GameDev Week project, and I am *not* about to be the first president of the club to make the annual event a total flop.' She waves the flash drive in front of my face for full effect.

I find my voice at last. 'Wait. You're part of the Much Dev Such Wow club too?'

'*President* of the Much Dev Such Wow club. Excuse you.' She winks at me, and for some reason, a tiny little butterfly comes alive in my chest. 'Are you here for the GameDev Week?'

'Umm, come to think of it, yeah, maybe.' I shove one hand into my pocket to act like I'm cool. 'The Dean called for me, and I don't know why, but I guess he's the mod or something?'

'He is. He's a geek,' Elle grins, and I notice she's got a very distinct chipped tooth that kind of makes her face even prettier

'So, you're a new recruit, huh? You don't happen to be that freshman who's weirdly into *Mitolohiya*, are you?'

I go red. 'What's wrong with *Mitolohiya*?'

'I knew it. I read your file from the member list.' She scrunches up her nose. 'You'd get along with my brother so damn well.'

And there it is—the six degrees of Kevin Bacon that connect the two of us, leading up to this very day. '*Mitolohiya* is the greatest game ever made,' I grin. 'My name is—'

'Hold up. Before you get all chummy with me, I want you to know that you're fraternizing with the enemy here.' She holds up her ID and taps at the bar underneath her name, telling me she is two years older than I am. 'I'm Elle, and when I graduate, I will work for Tala Tales Games' rival company.'

My eyes zero in on the ID in front of me, the letters of her name clearing into hyperfocus as everything else around it blurs and fades away.

Elle.

Elle.

My heart soars.

'Hi, Elle. I'm Nat.' I hold up my own ID hanging from my neck too, and I spot Elle eyeing the keychain dangling from it.

'*Co-ops for Life*, huh? Your girlfriend must be rooting for ya.'

I bite back a smile. The past few weeks made my heart lonelier, then stronger. The quiet static on my computer screen during late-night skirmishes no longer sent jolts of electricity through me, no longer reminded me of this thunderstorm of a girl who used to send the same sparks through my body. Over time, I found I was no longer looking over the monitor to see her pumping her fist into the air, no longer turning to my left to high-five a sweeping victory.

Lena has her own life now, and it's time for me to live mine.

I tilt my head at Elle, trying to be just as coy as she is. I hope it's working. 'She would, if I had one.'

'Hmm.' Elle twirls a finger around her lanyard and leans closer. 'It's just as well. No romantic partner would want to doom you to be her co-op for life, anyway.'

'That's true,' I say, like I've always known her even though we've never met. 'I mean, love isn't 50–50, right? It's flexible. When one goes thirty, the other goes seventy and vice versa. Love isn't a co-op, and you're not supposed to keep score to win any prize. It's not a game.'

'Sounds like you're speaking from experience.'

'If you call being a selfish, entitled idiot "experience", sure.' I grin. 'It's nice to meet you.'

'You sure you should be saying that?' She squints at me. 'I could be a spy sent to bring Tala Tales Games down, along with everything you hold dear.'

Tala Tales Games is still where I want to be, so it would be a shame if a corporate spy destroyed it from the inside, no matter how pretty she is. 'I'm sure. Didn't *The Art of War* say I should know my enemy and know myself?'

'Quoting Sun Tzu. The mark of a true real-time-strategy player.' She nods. 'You're interesting, recruit. Don't be late for the club's first meeting this afternoon.'

And with that, she spins on her heel and marches right out of the Dean's office before I can even respond.

'Nathaniel Carpio?'

I almost jump at the sound of Mrs Rodriguez's smiling voice behind me. 'The Dean will see you now.'

'Oh. Umm. Okay. Thank you.' I start toward the secretary's desk with a hand on my ID and half my soul out the door, my heart sinking, torn between Mrs Rodriguez waiting for me and this awesome, whirlwind of a girl who holds the power to bring down a company single-handedly.

Or so she says.

And when my meeting with the Dean is over, I want to get to know her better beneath all that she is and what she can do, and I kind of want to stick around to find out.

'Sorry,' I mumble to Mrs Rodriguez. 'If you could just give me one second? Just one sec—'

I spin around so fast that I almost trip out the door. The campus looms large and alive at me, as I whip left and right, trying to catch a whiff of that spunky pixie cut and the girl who might just ruin my future.

Then I see her. A little way to my right, Elle is leaning against a tree and stooping down to tie the shoelaces on her Chucks, like the RNG gods are in my favour and she took that exact moment and that exact tree and that exact amount of time to stop and wait for me to spot her in a sea of usernames and random pixels. Like I've always been in the Tutorial mode my whole life and this very moment will finally make me step out onto Stage One. Like I've only started to write my own code as I go along because life is always changing and evolving, and it's big and scary and awesome and real.

Like I can change my own ones and zeroes and maybe even level up along the way.

So, just like my very first 'Hello World' code, something clicks and opens up to me, and I run to her and tell her the words that will mark this moment in history as the moment I clear my not-to-epic NPC quest completely.

'You wanna go grab some lunch?'

* * *

END

Acknowledgements

In the strictest sense of the word, *For the Win: The Not-So-Epic Quest of a Non-Playable Character* is not a romance. There is no happily ever after, and my characters don't ride off into the sunset hand-in-hand with the promise of getting married and having kids. On the other end of the spectrum, it's not a depressing tragedy, either. *For the Win* is, in essence, a simple but realistic romp through the perils of young love and the misconceptions the youth often have along the way.

Despite the geeky gaming vibe that I know and love, it hasn't been the easiest story to tell, mainly because I struggled a lot with portraying the tricky waters of Nat's misguided 'love' here. This is exactly why my eternal gratitude goes out to my early beta readers, who read this first—when it was still titled *Confessions of a Low-Level NPC*—and helped shape it into what it is today: KB Meniado and Miel Salva, the undying combo I am indebted to, Stef Tran, Kayce Teo, Jinji Quiambao, Michael Recto, and Joyce Fernandez.

To Liana Bautista who made initial edits to the first draft back in early 2020, thank you for pointing out all of the red flags from the get-go. My limitless thanks go out once again to Bryce King who never fails to lawyer up for me—I still owe him coffee; to my ever-enthusiastic BFF Stephanie Sia whose support is only ever matched by her love for me, which I don't deserve; to my childhood friend Iris Siy who still buys every single book I write without fail—I'm not worthy; and to my closest friends who never miss a beat when it comes to cheering me on and believing in me even when I don't believe in myself.

Thank you to my beautifully brilliant Scribe Tribe—Kayce Teo, Joyce Chua, and Eva Wong Nava—who always rejoice and lament with me and who never tire of this shared rollercoaster ride; to the amazing Joyce Chng, E. L. Shen, Daryl Kho, Lena Jeong, Grace K. Shim, Lyn Liao Butler, and Anne Elicaño-Shields for sneaking blurbs for me into their ultra-hectic schedules (I look up to you all and will forever be grateful); to my fellow Penguin novelists and support group Marga Ortigas, Danton Remoto, and the entire PRH SEA author circle; to Melvin Choo and Dots Ngo for always squeezing out every ounce of effort to make sure our books are available out there despite the uphill battle.

My heartfelt appreciation goes out to the tireless family at Penguin Random House SEA: Thatchaa whose encouragement and passion for my words not only hone my story but also help me find my often-elusive confidence in myself; Garima and Chai who are honestly bottomless wells of love, positivity, and endless support; Alkesh, Ishani, Almira, and Pallavi for being the ultimate Dream Team when it comes to championing us; Nora for being our loving PRH mother who opened up her heart for us to tell our stories in the first place.

Of course, I wouldn't be able to do any of this without my family—my parents and my brother and my husband who love me and think I'm cool even though I'm just an NPC. To the #romanceclass and BRUMultiverse family—thank you all from the bottom of my heart.

As always, I owe it all to the Big Guy up there.

Most of all, thank you, dearest reader, for sticking by this odd little tale. It's a simple story about a gamer's quest for love that develops into a quiet but poignant account of what it means to find yourself. It tackles issues on learning to change and let go, as well as the right and wrong kind of love. While there's a lesson to be learned in there somewhere, I also just wanted to feed my geekiness by writing about video games, as always. *Mitolohiya*, in particular, is very much inspired by *StarCraft*, and is basically my wish that someone out there would make an actual RTS game about Filipino myths.

If nothing else, I do hope that you enjoyed the quirkiness of the tale and its emotional undertones, and maybe helped you appreciate—or reminisce about—young love in all its messy glory.

Thank you, thank you, thank you. GG!

Book Club Questions

1. There is a pervading sense of longing and heartache throughout the whole book. How does this reflect the ups and downs of young love?
2. Which character did you relate to the most and why?
3. What are the symbolisms of the *Mitolohiya* tribes to Nat's personality? To Lena's?
4. How do Nat's "game concepts" reflect the stages of his character development in the story?
5. What do you think happens to Lena after the book's official ending? To Raf? To Josh?
6. What is the significance of the title? Did you find it meaningful? Why or why not?
7. What do you think is the main theme of the book?
8. How has Nat's family upbringing affected his personality? How about Lena's upbringing?
9. How has gaming shaped the way Nat views the world?
10. Were there times you disagreed with Nat's actions? What would you have done differently?
11. Looking at the story from Lena's perspective, do you agree or disagree with her actions?
12. What is the significance of the "Hello World" code to Nat's personal growth?
13. Why do you think Nat sees himself as an NPC or Non-Playable Character?
14. How do the very first scene and the very last scene tie together?
15. What do you think is the pivotal moment in Nat's story that made him change?
16. What scene resonated with you most on a personal level?

17. How did you feel about the ending?
18. In the end, what do you think it really means to "win Elena Dizon's heart"?

Student Exercises

1. Try to tell the story from Lena's point of view.
2. List down the most quotable quotes in your opinion.
3. Create your own soundtrack for the book.
4. Make an online scrapbook as a book report.
5. Recreate a scene using art.
6. Which video games would you play with Nat?
7. Which movies would you recommend for Mr Dizon?
8. Notice how the book is sectioned into three "stages": destroy Rafael Antonio, level up, and win Elena Dizon's heart. Explain how this reflects the Three-Act Structure.